WAR CHI...

Varied experiences in t...
of Independence seen ... ...ung
people. Whelan's deep k... ...edge of this period in
Irish history, together with his sharp and accurate
dialogue and his strong sense of humanity and
humour, provide us with exceptional insights and an
authentic feeling for the plight of children in wartime.

GERARD WHELAN was born in Enniscorthy, County Wexford, where he now lives. He is the author of several books for children and is a multiple award-winner. His first novel, *The Guns of Easter*, won a Bisto Merit Award and the Eilís Dillon Memorial Award for first-time writers; *Dream Invader* was the overall winner of the Bisto Book of the Year Award.

Other books by Gerard Whelan
The Guns of Easter
A Winter of Spies
Dream Invader
Out of Nowhere

War Children

Children

GERARD WHELAN

THE O'BRIEN PRESS
DUBLIN

First published 2002 by The O'Brien Press Ltd,
20 Victoria Road, Dublin 6, Ireland.
Tel: +353 1 4923333; Fax: +353 1 4922777
E-mail: books@obrien.ie
Website: www.obrien.ie
Reprinted 2003.

ISBN: 0-86278-776-9

British Library Cataloguing-in-Publication Data
Whelan, Gerard
War children
1.Young adult fiction 2.Ireland - History - 1910-1921 - Fiction
I.Title
823.9'14[J]

2 3 4 5 6 7 8 9 10
03 04 05 06 07 08

Editing, typesetting, layout, design: The O'Brien Press Ltd
Cover image: every effort has been made to trace the copyright holder,
without success; should they contact us we will be glad to hear from them.
Printing: Cox & Wyman Ltd

DEDICATION

In memory of my sorely missed aunt, Kathleen Doyle – dancer, chainsmoker, fabulist, teetotaller, black humorist, practical joker, and dedicated stewer of strong, strong tea.

ACKNOWLEDGEMENTS

Various people have read and made helpful comments on
this material at various times, among whom I should
(as ever!) single out Liz Morris and Frank Murphy in particular.
My special thanks are due to Mark O'Sullivan,
for practical assistance with the linguistic plumbing
at the end of 'Mulligan's Drop'.

Note

We in Ireland tend to describe the events that happened here in the years before 1921 as a 'war of independence', but this is not what it was called at the time. It was especially hard for the British to call it that, since politically – like other colonial powers later on in the twentieth century – they had to deny there was a war going on at all. While Ireland was legally part of the United Kingdom, and had British troops in it just as other parts of the UK did, the Government solution to the problem was to call the guerrilla fighters criminals and to militarise the police force. To strengthen the backbone of the old **Royal Irish Constabulary**, two new 'police' units were recruited, mainly from soldiers left over from the recently-ended First World War. One of these forces was known as the **Auxiliaries** (called '**Auxies**' for short by the Irish) and was made up of former officers. The other force, whose members acquired a fearsome reputation that has remained to this day, were universally known by the nickname they were given by the Irish. The new force was mustered in such a hurry that there weren't enough proper police uniforms for them, and in their early days they were dressed in mixture of the dark green RIC uniform and army khaki; because of this they were nicknamed, after a famous pack of hunting dogs, the **Black and Tans**.

The Empty Steps

I was standing in the kitchen when there was a knock at the back door, and when I opened it Mattie Foley stuck a pistol in my face.

'Hands up, Nancy!' she growled in a let-on tough man's voice.

I suppose I let a squeal out of me. My Ma, who was kneading dough at the kitchen table, looked up and gasped at what she saw.

'Matilda Foley!' she said, in a tough voice that wasn't a bit let-on. 'You put that thing down *now*!'

Mattie giggled and, holding the gun high, wafted past me into the kitchen. I stood looking after her, with my hand still on the handle of the door. Ma held her flour-covered hand out to Mattie.

'Give me that,' she said. 'Is it real? Where did you get it?'

Mattie hesitated. For a second she looked like she was going to refuse, then she handed Ma the gun.

'I found it in the yard by the back wall,' she said. 'It's real enough. I bet some gunman got caught in the street search this morning, and thrun it in over the wall so it wouldn't be found on him.'

The soldiers and Auxies had blocked both entrances to the court and searched everyone and everywhere. They hadn't bothered saying who or what they were looking for, but then they never did. At any rate they'd arrested nobody, just terrified everyone and made the usual nuisance of themselves. Still, no-one had been hurt, and not much broken. That was something.

Ma handled the gun like she might catch something off of it. She put it down very carefully on the table and stood with her hands on her hips looking down at it. Mattie stood beside her, wriggling her whole body the way she did whenever she was excited. She rubbed each bare, dirty foot in turn along the ankle of the other, like she always did too. It made people laugh the way she could never stand still. Her nickname was 'Dancer' because of it – and to rhyme with her Da's nickname, which was 'Chancer', because that's what he was, a complete chancer.

I shut the back door and went over beside Ma and Mattie. We all stood and looked at the gun. It looked evil, and it looked twice as evil there on the floury table beside the big ordinary lump of everyday dough.

'That's a Mauser,' Mattie said. She liked to know the names of things.

The gun really was an ugly-looking thing. It was a big black metal rectangle with a rounded butt sticking out of it and a long, thin, nearly delicate-looking barrel.

'How do you know it's a Mauser?' Ma said. 'It could be a Maxim gun for all you know.'

But Mattie pointed to some words stamped proud on the metal just above the wooden grips.

'See here,' she said, and read slowly: '*Waffen ... fabrik Mauser ... Oberndorf ... A. Neckar*. That's German, that is.'

I'd never seen German writing before, any more than Mattie had. But I took her word for it. The word Mauser was plain to see, and everybody knew that they were German guns. The German rifles the rebels had used in the Rising had been Mausers. There was an old fellow in the court who'd been out in '16, and he called the rifles 'Lousers' because he said they were rotten guns and nearly took the arm off you every time you fired one.

Mattie was very proud of being able to read. She was the first in her family to have learned. But it seemed little use when the words were in a foreign language. At least German seemed to be written with real letters – not like Irish, that was supposed to be our own language but was written in a mad alphabet that only a few odd-bods could make out.

Ma's eyes weren't the best. She leaned down and squinted at the printing on the gun.

'It says Mauser, all right,' she said. 'But the rest is gibberish to me. *Waffenfabrik* – what class of a fabric might that be, I wonder? *Oberndorf* sounds like a place. But *A. Neckar* – that's like someone's name.'

'I bet you it's the fella that made it!' Mattie said. 'Oh, I wonder what he's like! What could the "*A*" stand for? Not Archie, surely. Alfred, maybe. No – it'd be a foreign name.'

'Anthony,' I suggested.

Mattie wrinkled up her face.

'Sure that's not foreign, Nancy. I know – Antonio! Antonio Neckar! And he puts his name on every gun he makes, because he's proud of it.'

And she started to sing, which she'd do at the slightest excuse:

> '*Oh, Oh, Antonio,*
> *He's gone away.*
> *Left me alone-io,*
> *All on my own-io.*'

But Ma became very serious.

'Shut up, Mattie,' she said. 'This is bad.'

She slapped the gun with the flat of her hand. 'Don't you know what this is?' she said.

Mattie looked puzzled. 'A Mauser pistol,' she said. 'Made in Oberndorf out of Waffenfabrik by Herr Antonio Neckar, the master gunsmith.'

It was as if Ma didn't hear her. Ma's face was suddenly tight and hard.

'It's a death-sentence for any man in the house that it's found in,' she snapped. Now the gun looked even more ugly, and I got a cold feeling in my stomach thinking of my

Da and of my brothers Jim and Ray. They were at work now, but they were all old enough to be suspicious characters to the Tans. There were boys my own age throwing bombs at the Tans in their tenders – fourteen-year-old boys, trying to kill soldiers! Succeeding, sometimes, too. I looked again at the gun. It seemed to have got bigger as well as uglier.

'We have to get it out of here,' Ma said.

'There's no need to say "we", Mrs Ryan,' Mattie said. 'It's not your problem: I found it, remember.'

Her voice sounded mild, which meant Ma was trying her temper.

If Mattie had one fault it was that she couldn't share things. Her Da was a complete waster, and drank what little money he got. Any money her Ma made skivvying went on the rent. They never had enough to eat, never any proper clothes – their good clothes, as my Da said, were the ones that had patches on the holes in them. That kind of poverty made you greedy, Da used to say; it made you greedy whether you were that way by nature or not. The Foleys had so little that they didn't feel able to share even their troubles – and with Chancer Foley for a Da, troubles was the one thing they'd more than enough of. He'd been picked out of more gutters, my Da used to say, than a fag-butt.

Mattie picked the Mauser up off our table. It looked even bigger in her little hands. We were almost exactly the same age, but Mattie was tiny. She looked at the gun and she smiled.

'Maybe I'll just leave it back where I got it,' she said.

'No,' said Ma. 'It's too late for that now. If it's found there then all the men and the older lads will be arrested – at the very least.'

'Sure, who'll find it?' Mattie said. 'They raided only this morning, and they never even looked in the yard. They won't be back this way for a while.'

It hadn't struck me that the pistol had been in the yard while the Auxies were around. Thinking of that now I was suddenly frightened.

'You can't leave it there,' Ma said. 'For all we know they could raid again tomorrow – and this time they might look there. And what will we do if they don't – leave it for your little brothers and sisters to play with?'

'I'll keep it somewhere safe, so,' Mattie said. 'I've a secret place where I keeps things.'

I wondered what place could be secret in that house teeming with children. Mattie was the eldest of ten brothers and sisters. And her Da, Chancer, had a nose for anything that might be turned into drink-money.

'It's worse in the house,' Ma said. 'Don't you understand that? They'll be sure it's your Da's if they find it.'

Mattie thought, but then she giggled – that was Mattie's problem, I suppose: she saw the funny side of everything. But it was what made you like her as well.

'A raid would sober Da up,' Mattie said. 'That would be a sight to see. I wouldn't know him if I saw him sober.'

'That thing has to be got out of here altogether,' Ma said.

'And what if it's gone,' Mattie said, 'and its owners come looking for it? What do we tell them?'

Ma's hand went up to her mouth. You could see she hadn't thought of that. She was as frightened of crossing the gunmen as of crossing the British. All you wanted to do in them days was keep your head down, and hope no-one hit it. Even that didn't always work.

Mattie looked at the gun. 'I'll get rid of it some way,' she said in the reasonable, sincere voice that told me she was lying. 'I'll stuff it down a shorehole or something. If the gunmen do come then I'll say I never saw it. They'll blame one of the childer. Anyway,' she said, 'I suppose we can all guess whose it is.'

Ma said nothing to that, but I knew we were all thinking of the mystery man who was staying in Nolans'. He'd been there for a week now, a dark young man who came and went. Mrs Nolan gave it out that he was a cousin of theirs from Fairview that was looking for lodgings, but his whole manner suggested something else. No-one in the whole court doubted that he was some class of gunman, probably on the run. Naturally no-one would say anything, because we weren't like that. Certainly no-one would tell anyone official. It's not that we were mad rebels or anything, but 'informer' was about the dirtiest word you could call anyone. Our sort were natural enemies of the police, because they were natural enemies of ours. My Da had explained all that to me: the police were on the side of them that had things; they were there to protect them from them that had nothing – the likes of us. If the rebels won, and Ireland got its own police, we'd be their enemies too. It was just the way things were.

Mattie said no more, but turned towards the door.

'Oh God, don't walk around outside with that, Mattie, love,' Ma said.

But Mattie smiled at her. She'd a lovely smile.

'Sure, who's to see me in the yard?' she said. She posed in the doorway with a hand on her hip, the pistol held up by her ear.

'Look, Nancy,' she said. 'I'm Countess Markievicz during the Rising.'

Her face assumed what she supposed was a Countess's look. It made her look a bit like a codfish. I was going to laugh, but Mattie couldn't keep it up: she herself laughed first. Then she went out into the yard, still holding the gun.

'She's a terrible young one, that Mattie,' Ma said, but she said it fondly. Mattie had a hard life at home, and Ma pitied her. Mattie's Ma was her best friend. Our houses backed on to one another, sharing a yard that was enclosed on two sides by a high stone wall. There'd been a tanyard years ago where our houses stood, and the wall was all that was left of it. That and a tanyard smell, Mattie used to say, though I never smelled it myself. I think she just meant it smelled bad. I suppose it did, but there were worse places.

Maybe Mattie really did smell the tanyard in her mind. They talk about 'the mind's eye' so I suppose you could have a mind's nose too. If so, then Mattie Foley was the sort of person who'd have one. She was a funny girl. She had a great imagination, and was always making up very compli-cated stories that would go on forever. She'd tell you these stories, and she was so convincing that you'd half-believe her even though you knew they weren't true. I think she half-believed them herself. My Ma used to say that Mattie lived in her imagination; I suppose it was better than living with Chancer Foley.

Our houses were the only two left standing from an old row of back-to-back cottages in a cramped court in the centre of the city. The other houses had fallen or been pulled down, and they'd been replaced by a new row of hovels even more densely packed together. The newer houses were in even worse condition than our older ones. That was what came of cheap building, my Da said – cheap building and cheating gangers.

Both our house and Mattie's were owned by the same landlord. He was something in the city corporation. We never saw him, only his agent that came for the rent money. The cottages were very old, and we lived there only because we couldn't live anywhere else. Nobody in their right mind would live in such a place, given a choice.

My brother Jim had started working as a messenger boy that spring. Now that there were three wages coming into the house Da wanted to move. He wanted us to live somewhere better. Mattie was always asking me whether we'd found a place yet. She hoped it wasn't far away, she said; she didn't want to lose her only friend.

'But, Mattie,' I'd say, 'sure, you're the most popular girl in the street. Even old Mrs Curran the monster likes you, and she don't like anyone.'

'Ah, Nancy,' Mattie would say, 'they likes me, but they don't understand me. You and me, Nan, we're two of a kind.'

And we *were* best friends, although calling us two of a kind was plain daft. I could never be like her: I was too timid. Mattie was mad as a hatter – 'harum-scarum' my Ma called it. Not that Ma didn't like Mattie – everybody liked her, that was true; but Ma was certainly glad that she didn't have to live with her. Ma would have murdered me if I'd got into quarter as much trouble as Mattie did. But Mattie's Ma was always working, and her Da was always drunk; my Ma never blamed her for the trouble that she got in, only pitied her. People found excuses for Mattie, however she managed it.

'She's the most unfortunate class of an orphan,' Ma would say. 'The kind whose Ma and Da are still alive.'

I didn't see much of Mattie the rest of that day or the next, which was odd. She had to mind the rest of the Foley brood, of course, but otherwise she was usually as much a fixture in the street as a lamp-post – well, there were no lamp-posts in the court, but you know what I mean. We kids lived in the streets then, and the adults too. The streets were healthier, anyway, than the houses we lived in.

I wondered about Mattie and I wondered about the pistol. I kept an eye out for the young man from Nolans' but I didn't see him either. Then the next evening I was playing chasing with some kids at our corner when I saw Mattie walking along. I ran straight over to her.

'Where were you?' I asked her. 'I didn't see you since yesterday.'

Mattie gave me an odd smile. She took my wrist and led me over to what we called the Empty Steps. These were a set of six wide stone steps that had once – we supposed – led up to the front door of a house. It must have been a very long time ago. At any rate the house was so long gone that nobody could remember anything about it. Nothing was left except these stone steps going nowhere. They were used for playing on, and to hang washing on, but mostly as a seat. Mattie pulled me down on them now, still holding my wrist in her thin fingers. There was a sort of intensity in her grip.

'I was away,' she said mysteriously.

'Away?' The very idea was strange. Round our way,

when you said that someone was away then you usually meant they were in jail.

'Away with my *man*,' Mattie said.

That one flummoxed me altogether. I stood there with my mouth open. Mattie smiled at the look on my face.

'My man Antonio,' she said, and I knew where I was then: Mattie was off on one of her fantasies. I could fill in a lot of the details, because I'd heard them so often before – the neat little house where she'd live with her devoted man, making him sandwiches and sending him off to work. Lots of girls had daydreams, but Mattie's were special: they were very detailed, and she told them in that voice that made me think she half-believed them herself. I wouldn't class them as lies. They were fictions, like people make up and put in books.

A thing I'd noticed about Mattie's fantasies too was that in a strange way they were very ordinary. My other friends fantasised about living in palaces and having servants, of being rich or famous or married to a prince; Mattie's dreams were of much simpler things. Maybe that was partly what made them sound so real. One time when I told my Ma about one of Mattie's stories, Ma got a soft, sad look on her face.

'A clean house and a decent man and something to put in a sandwich,' Ma said, 'is as big a dream to a girl like Mattie as any palace.'

It was that way now, in the story Mattie told me on the

Empty Steps. This time Mattie lived in Germany. She lived with Antonio Neckar in a little rose-covered cottage with a garden where Mattie grew vegetables. They had lovely sofa-coverings and curtains made of the softest, finest *Waffenfabrik*. ('I figured it out, Nancy,' she said. '*Waffen* means weaving: doesn't it sound like it? *Waffenfabrik* is woven fabric – that lovely soft sort of stuff that they puts on cushions and armchairs.')

Mattie made sausage sandwiches every morning for Antonio's dinner, and sent him out to work with a little package of them under his arm in brown paper. He'd sit at his table in the factory and assemble pistols, thinking all the time of his dear Mattie and determined to make good guns that would help her poor homeland be free.

'He have trouble with his eyes,' Mattie told me, 'because some of the parts in the pistols is very small and he spends all day squinting at all the little springs and bits. And he gets headaches sometimes when he comes home of an evening, from all the squinting, and I bathes his poor forehead with a damp cloth. He've a lovely high forehead – a noble forehead. And sometimes when I'm wiping his poor head he'll put his hand on mine and we just stays there, him in his favourite armchair and me standing over him, saying nothing, happy, listening to the German band playing out in the square.'

Mattie always got a look in her eyes when she was telling a story like that. A faraway look. She wasn't seeing the dirty court with its piles of rubbish, or the barefoot kids in their castoff clothes and their scabs. She was, I knew, seeing the place she described. She was in a kind of a trance. And I often longed just once to glimpse the places that she saw, for all that they were never palaces. Because when I looked around all I saw was what was there, and what was there wasn't a whole lot to look at.

I suppose I should have quizzed Mattie about the pistol. I knew her too well to think she'd have told me anything if she didn't want to, but still I should have asked. I'd have felt better after. Because Mattie's stories took her over in a way, and she got ... impractical, I suppose, is the best word for it. And in lives like ours, and in days like them days especially, impractical was one thing that you just couldn't afford to get. Mattie's dreams were powerful, and Mattie's dreams were nice; but they were dreams. In the real world, like the Empty Steps they led nowhere.

My Ma had said nothing to my Da about the Mauser, and she'd warned me to keep quiet too.

'There's no point in worrying him,' she said to me. 'I only hope Mattie have the sense to dump it someplace. The best we can all do is forget we ever saw it.'

I agreed with her completely, but I had a bad feeling about that gun. To Mattie, now, it was a sort of memento of Antonio. I'd seen her get like that about odd things before. There was one time that we found a little hip-flask in the gutter in Elliot Place. It was early one morning when we were on our way back from looking for the loose coal on the quays. A few lumps used always fall off the wagons bringing the unloaded coal to the yards, and you'd always see women and children there scavenging for them. It was all the fuel that some people had – unless they burned the furniture, which most of them had done long ago anyhow, if they'd ever had any furniture.

But oh, that flask! Mattie kept it for days. It became part of one of her oddest fantasies, about a young doctor who loved the poor. This doctor had invented a cure for consumption, the great scourge of the slums. There was only one batch of the cure and he'd kept it in the flask for safety. He'd been attacked while he was answering an emergency call, and he'd beaten off his attackers but dropped the flask. Now he was lying hurted in one of the city hospitals, despairing of ever finding again the cure he couldn't duplicate. Mattie would keep it safe for him, hiding it from thieves and from other, evil doctors who'd steal his discovery.

I knew myself that the flask was for holding drink. You could see a dozen like it in the window of Peterson's shop. But the power of Mattie's stories was so strong that I started looking out for strangers in the court, especially for anyone who looked like an unscrupulous doctor. They'd have been easy to spot there, God knows: doctors didn't come anywhere near the likes of us.

Anyway Mattie had managed to hide the flask somewhere, but Chancer Foley, her Da, came across it. He lost

his rag when he found it had no drink in it, but then he realised the flask was silver and could be sold. When Mattie
found he'd sold it she nearly went mad herself. The odd
thing was, the way she ranted you could see that in some
way she really believed her own fantasy. Chancer had acted
as an agent for one of the evil doctors, she said. He'd
betrayed her young hero and cheated the poor of a cure for
a disease that plagued them. Was there anything he
wouldn't do for drink? Now he'd sold human life for
drink-money, and he'd pay for it in hell!

It would have been all right if she'd talked like that to
me. But she'd screamed it at Chancer himself as he drank
with his cronies in a pub – spending the few shillings he'd
got for the flask.

When he couldn't shut her up, and the landlord told
him to get out if he couldn't control her, Chancer flared up
in a drunken rage. He kicked Mattie out into the street and
there and then he gave her a beating that was still talked of
in the court, even there where my own parents' habit of not
beating their children was looked on as something strange
and nearly sinful.

'You won't dance for a while now, Dancer,' Chancer
Foley raged, kicking Mattie as she lay dazed and bleeding in
the dirt of the street. 'You won't dance around screaming at
a poor man in his misery!'

In the end, some of the men had pulled him off before
he killed her. Chancer had a terrible temper when he was

drunk, at least with his wife and children. I was amazed that Mattie had crossed him in his cups, but even more when I heard the things she'd said. It was as though the fantasy was so strong that she'd forgotten the reality. Like I say, she was impractical.

When I got my Ma on her own that night, after I'd talked to Mattie on the Empty Steps, I told her the latest.

'She have that gun someplace still, Ma,' I said. 'She have it hid – I'm sure of it.'

Ma looked worried, but there was nothing we could do. Mattie was a wild thing.

The next morning, just after eight o'clock, the Auxies and the soldiers came back. They blocked the entrances to the court as they'd done two mornings before, and they got off their lorries and stood around with bayonets fixed on their rifles. The soldiers weren't too bad, but the Auxies must have been specially picked for their bad tempers. Kids would go up to the friendlier-looking Tommies and ask them questions – what they were looking for and so on – and sometimes they'd answer and they'd crack a joke. But from the Auxies you'd get a curse at best, and more often a kick. They drank too much, my Da said: every morning started off for them with a hangover.

When they were all in place that day a last police tender drove in. In the back there were more Auxies and a forlorn-looking figure who was obviously a prisoner. He was dressed in a white shirt that was torn and bloody, and his face was puffed and bruised and bloody too from being beaten. When they threw him off the back of the lorry he landed on his back and cried out in pain, clutching one shoulder with a bloody hand. My heart went out to him, the way your heart would go out to any hurted thing. But at the same time a part of me wished that he'd drop stone dead where he stood. Because even under the bruising and the swelling I recognised the man: it was the stranger who'd been staying in Nolans', the one we'd thought must own the gun.

I'd been in the street when I saw the first tenders come into the court, and I'd wondered whether to run home or to stay and watch. When I saw the prisoner I was doubly torn, not knowing what to do. The Auxies drove the man on with cuffs and riflebutts to Nolans', where old Mrs Nolan was standing in the doorway with her apron up to her mouth, looking in horror at the poor face of her lodger coming towards her. The Tans pushed him in the door, and her too, and followed them in. There was a great noise of things breaking, and a lot of cursing. A woman's voice screamed in anguish, and a man's in pain. Then the prisoner was flung out the door again; he landed in the street with a big groan and a fresh bloody place on his face.

People stood around, frozen, watching. I was frozen too. I think in my heart I knew what was coming next, but I didn't want to know. A half-dozen doors down from Nolans' was a high wall, and behind that wall was the back yard we shared with the Foleys. The bloodied man was walking down the street towards the wall. He staggered like a drunken man, hardly able to stand upright, holding his maimed shoulder, leaving drops of blood on the cobbles as he went. A half-dozen Auxies walked around him, grim and silent now, watching him, prodding him on with bayonets.

When the man reached the wall he stopped and put his back to it. He slid slowly down till he was sitting in the street. He wept. We all stood looking. You could feel the people's pity. Most of us had no truck with rebels or rebelling, but this was only a hurted man crying. The Auxies had had him; and you wouldn't wish that on your worst enemy.

One of the Auxies barked at the man.

'Well?' he said. 'Was it here?'

It wasn't an English accent, or even a Scottish one. Maybe it was Canadian or American. There was all sorts in the Auxies.

The weeping man nodded his head.

'It was,' he said, and the two words were a sob.

The Auxie who'd spoken turned to his men. 'Get that damned gun,' he said. 'And I don't care if you have to tear down every house in the place.'

At once the Auxies were running round both ends of the wall, heading for the houses that backed onto the yard. My house. Mattie's house. My heart was in my mouth. I knew they'd destroy everything in our house, but there wasn't so much to destroy. It wasn't things I was worried about: it was Mattie.

I was torn between a longing to run home and a longing to stay where I could see it all. I knew my Ma would be worried about me, but she'd be glad I wasn't home. They would go through our house like a whirlwind, and they'd break what they could break; but at least she'd be safe in the knowledge that there was nothing dangerous there. With me on her hands she'd only worry more.

I told myself this, but still I wondered. From our house I could try to get into the yard. I could try to see what was happening with Mattie. I'd no idea where her secret place was, but I was certain that the pistol would be there. If the Auxies found it there was no telling what they'd do. Chancer Foley would make the most unlikely suspect as a gunman that I could imagine; but unlikely men had been shot as gunmen already, and men and boys shot without any hint of suspicion at all.

Some people made a move to follow in the direction the Auxies had gone, to see what was happening. But the soldiers and the other Auxies kept us all back, watching us for signs of suspicious movements. Harmless-looking men had pulled out guns before in situations like this, and started blazing away at them. It wasn't simple brutality, I should say that for them. They had to be careful.

Then there was shouting, and a small figure came flying

around the

dancing feet run...

figures of Auxies ran a... high wall. It was Mattie, with her

all because I'd seen what Mat... hair flying behind her. Dark

its butt with her two little hands: ...had no eyes for them at

of Antonio, the cursed Mauser. ...rying, holding it by

...black memento

One of the waiting Auxies made a grab ... ...r and missed. She screamed at him to leave her alone. Mo... of them tried to pen her in, but she wrong-footed them with those dancing feet, dodging around them and in and out of groups of bystanders, leading her pursuers a merry dance. People shied away from her as she neared them – shied away not from her but from that ugly black thing she was holding in her hands. The Auxies and soldiers were shouting and cursing, a dozen of them or more pushing towards her and getting mixed up with locals and shoving them out of the way.

I don't know what Mattie thought she was doing. She must have known the entrances to the court would be blocked. There was never a way out for her, and the place was crawling with British.

An Auxie caught Mattie's shoulder. She smashed his hand away with the pistol and he cursed. Mattie danced off again. She reached the Empty Steps and she danced up them to the top. Then she just stood there, breathing hard. She looked up and out around the broken-backed roofs of the court, peered at all the faces turned towards her as

though looking for some... just backed away and
No-one said a wo... British too had quietened,
watched this mad ...ow, a big circle of khaki and black
knowing they bgged creature on the Empty Steps – my
surrounding...ne of them taking their eyes off her, none of
best frie...king their eyes off the death in her hands.
them

Antonio!' Mattie shouted, really loud.

She did. I heard her.

I can hear her still.

She should never have raised the gun. All the rest she might have got away with. If she'd got a beating itself, sure, it wouldn't have been the first she'd had. They mightn't have believed she knew nothing, but they wouldn't have tortured a child. Maybe they would if they'd been let, I don't know; but surely they wouldn't have been let torture a young girl.

But she did raise the gun, and she pointed it at a soldier, and she squeezed the trigger.

There was a very loud click as the hammer fell. No bang, just a very loud click sounding in the total silence. Maybe it was a misfire. Maybe the pistol was empty. But it didn't fire.

The British guns did. Three, four, maybe half a dozen of them. All I heard was a ragged volley, swollen by the echoes from the crowded houses in that mean square, and Mattie Foley was raised up off the Empty Steps with the force of the bullets. It seemed to happen very slowly. The Dancer

Foley's feet did a last little flurry in the air, and her skinny body wriggled with the force of bullets. She spun around completely. Then she fell in a little bundle of nothing and tumbled down to lie in the dirt at the foot of the steps.

I felt like I'd been shot myself. It didn't hurt, but it was like a big lump of lead had been slammed into my chest and stayed stuck there. I felt like I was sinking into the ground with the weight of it. The women started keening and the men started cursing and the children started crying. They all started running away, as if they expected the soldiers and Auxies to mow them all down now. Stranger things had happened. I just stood there looking at Mattie. The British closed in around her, and all I could see was the odd flash of rags through gaps between their boots. Someone who was crying and saying broken words grabbed me and hustled me off. I fought them, fought to stay where I could see my friend. But the person was too strong. When we got around the corner of the high wall I looked to see who it was. It was my Ma.

Our house wasn't broken up too bad. Mattie had made her run with the gun before the Tans got properly started on it. Ma sat me down at the kitchen table, but I started shivering so hard in my whole body that my knees bounced off the bottom of the table. I think I had some kind of a fit. I know that I fell on the ground and I was shaking and then I was gone. When I woke up I was lying in the bed with an overcoat over me and Ma was bathing my forehead with cold water from the bucket. She was crying without making any noise.

'The poor child,' she kept saying. 'The poor, poor child.'

I suppose she was talking about Mattie. Maybe she was talking about me. She tried to get me talking but I hadn't the heart to say anything. There didn't seem to be anything to say. After a long time she left me alone in the room with the curtains pulled and I lay in the dark and I stared at nothing. I didn't actually cry at all. I just stared. I don't know what I thought about – nothing, I think, if you can think about nothing. Little rose-covered cottages and sofas covered with *Waffenfabrik* and sausage sandwiches, maybe. Antonio Neckar with his headaches and his squinty eyes.

My Da came in to me that night when he got home.

'Nancy,' he said, 'would you not come out and talk to us?'

He put a hand on my shoulder and I held it. He worked on the docks, my Da. He was a big strong man but I never heard him say a cross word to one of us kids unless he had to. One time a man blamed my brother Ray for breaking his window. He blamed Ray because Ray was outside when the man came out to see who'd done it. Ray swore he hadn't but the man wanted to take it out on somebody. He was boxing Ray's head when Da came up and asked Ray if he'd broken the window. Again Ray said he hadn't. The man called Ray a liar, and still tried to hit him. Da hit the man a single box that left him stretched out on the street with his jaw broke.

'When you call my son a liar,' he said to the man, 'then you call me a liar. I may not have much but I have my word. Don't try and take it away from me.'

Afterwards I found out that Ray really had broken the window, but he was ashamed to tell Da because he'd have been disappointed. Years later, when Da was dying, Ray, a grown man then, confessed that thing to him. Da laughed.

'Sure, I knew you were after doing it,' he said to Ray. 'But that fellow was only a bully. And I never liked bullies.'

When I held my Da's hand that night, the time Mattie Foley got shot, that's when I started to cry. I cried and I cried and I shook the same way I'd been shaking at the kitchen table. Da held me tight till the sobbing went down, then he brought me out and sat me down and Ma gave me a cup of sweet tea. Jim and Ray were sitting by the fire. No-one said anything. We were sitting like that for a while when there was a knock on the door. My Da opened it and two men were standing there. They were strangers.

'Well?' Da said.

'We're asking around about a friend of ours,' one of the men said. He spoke with a country accent.

Da looked at them for a long while.

'Come in,' he said then, and they came in past him. They were young men in caps, with long dark coats. They looked serious and shifty at the same time. I was too numb to take them in, really, but I could sense the others tensing. Da closed the door and came over to the table. He sat down and looked up at the men without asking them to sit.

'What do you want to know?' he asked.

'We had a friend staying with Mrs Nolan,' the man with the country accent said. 'He had a bit of a problem.'

'Someone informed on him,' the other man said impatiently. He was a Dub.

Da looked from one to the other.

'Well, it was no-one in this house,' he said. He sounded tired. 'We minds our own business, and we don't like peelers.'

'We believe,' the first man said, 'there was money involved.'

Da looked like he was going to spit, but Ma would have taken the head off him if he'd done it in the house.

'Blood money, so,' he said. 'No good ever came of blood money.'

There was a clatter on the back door, and I jumped. I must have made some noise too because Ma came over and held me. Da was on his feet facing the door with his fists clenched. Each of the strangers stuck a hand in a pocket of his topcoat.

The back door was always on the latch. It opened now and Chancer Foley came in. His face was white.

'Mick,' my Da said. 'I'm sorry for your trouble.'

Chancer Foley held up a silencing hand. He looked past my father at the two strangers.

'Youse are looking for the man that put your friend on the spot,' he said.

There was something odd about him that I couldn't place. Then I realised he wasn't drunk. Here was Chancer Foley sober – a sight Mattie had said she'd never seen.

The two young men looked at Chancer. They took their empty hands out of their pockets.

'What do you know about it?' the second one asked. He was thin-faced, intense.

Chancer Foley started crying. It was an ugly sight, without even drink to excuse it.

'I'm the man,' he said. 'I'm who you're looking for.'

I felt something like a lump of ice moving up and down my spine.

'I had a daughter,' Chancer said, 'and one time my daughter told me I'd do anything for drink-money. I'd sell human life for it, she said, and I'd pay for it in hell.'

His whole face was moving as he spoke, big spasms moving across it. His eyes were mad.

'Well, I done it!' he said. 'I sold human life for it. And she was right – I'm paying. But it's not enough.'

He looked over at my Da.

'She was a mad young one,' he said. 'Mad as a hatter. You could neither talk sense into her nor beat it into her. But she was only a young one, when all is said and done.

There was no harm in her.'

There was a drip on the end of Chancer's nose. He wiped it with his coat-sleeve.

'Them boyos the other day,' he said to the two men. 'The Auxies. They were looking for a man. They said they'd pay good money for word of strangers. And money is money.'

'Blood money,' my father said.

'Blood money, aye. I never knew what that meant.' Chancer held up two shaking hands, the dirty palms washed clean in places by the sweat and maybe tears on them.

'When I looks at these hands now,' he said, 'I sees them full of me own daughter's blood. It was on the street outside today, her blood. A big lock of it. Me wife had to go out and scrub it up when she came back from work. I found her still at it when I came home. She had the blood washed up this long time, there wasn't a sign of it on the stones. But she was still scrubbing. She'd scrub the very stones out of the ground on that spot if she could.'

He put his hands down and looked at the men.

'There's a stone wall outside here where this whole thing started.' he said. 'Your mate saw the Auxies coming the other morning, and he thrun the gun over the wall. I seen him do it. I wants youse to take me out now and put me up against that wall. I'm asking youse to do it. Begging youse. I'd do it me own self only I've nothing to do it with.'

The second stranger, the intense one, moved as if to go over to Chancer; but his friend stopped him.

'It was your daughter that was shot?' he asked quietly.

Chancer looked at him with mad eyes.

'Sure, what do you think I'm talking about?' he said. 'You stupid culchie!'

The young man looked at him evenly.

'I think,' he said, 'you've been punished enough.'

Chancer Foley moved quicker than I'd ever seen him move. He crossed the room and grabbed the man's coat by the lapels. He was taller and heavier than the countryman, and he glowered down at him.

'No!' he said. 'No, I haven't.'

The countryman reached up and pulled Chancer's hands from his coat. He looked up at him coldly.

'It's a priest you need,' he said. 'And I'm not a priest.'

He nodded to his friend. The two of them bade us goodnight and went out, closing the door after them. Chancer looked around at us. He started to say something to my Da, but something in Da's eyes stopped him. Chancer ran out the back door, leaving it open behind him. A couple of days later his body was fished out of Dublin bay by a dredger. There were no signs of violence.

*   *   *

The court where I grew up is gone now. There's a block of offices and apartments on the site. Well-dressed young men and women come and go, talking on their mobile phones, running busily up and down steps that are rarely empty. My mother and father are long gone to their reward. My brother Ray fought in the British army during the Hitler war. He died in Germany in 1945. My brother Jim went to America. I was over there last year for his funeral. I often think of Mattie, and wonder what would have become of her. One time when myself and my husband were home on a holiday we went to the National Museum. They've a special display there about them times, with guns and uniforms from the Rising and from the Tan war. There's an Auxie uniform there that set the hairs of my neck standing up when I saw it. But the thing that struck me most was a pistol, a Mauser pistol, there in a glass case. It was the spit and image of the one that Mattie Foley brought into our kitchen that morning. You could even see the same words stamped on the metal: *Waffenfabrik Mauser ... Oberndorf A. Neckar.* And for the first time in too many years I thought of Antonio Neckar, with his headaches and his craftsmanship.

There was a couple looking into the case at the same time as me, and when they spoke to each other I recognised the language as German. They even said something about Mausers – maybe surprised to find so many of the guns had come from their own country. And though it wasn't like me at all, I turned to the couple and asked them about the words stamped on the pistol, and I learned that *Waffenfabrik* wasn't a thing you'd cover sofas with at all, but that it just meant 'weapons factory'. And I learned too that the rest of the inscription meant only a factory site, *Oberndorf-Am-Neckar*, the Neckar being a river and Oberndorf-Am-Neckar being the same sort of a name as, say, Kingston-on-Thames, where my sister-in-law used to live. And, of course, it's not that I'd ever believed that there really was a fellow called Antonio Neckar, because I'd known all along it was only a mad story, but in a foolish kind of a way I found myself standing there not knowing whether to laugh or cry. Because, mad or not, Mattie Foley had called out to Antonio with her last living breath. And as we left the museum I seemed to hear a little girl's voice echoing in the high rooms, up in the rafters, singing a daft old song:

> '*Oh, Oh, Antonio,*
> *He's gone away.*
> *Left me alone-io,*
> *All on my own-io.*'

I think that, in a strange way, and though I hadn't thought about him for years, Antonio Neckar came alive a bit in my own mind that day. Because those things in the glass cases – the uniforms and the guns – they were only history, and history is a name for things that are dead. And Antonio, even though he'd never existed, was still more alive than those things. Because Antonio, with his headaches and his craft, like Mattie Foley with her dirty dancing feet, would never be a dead thing in a museum. The only

Mulligan's Drop

Statia's father had twisted his ankle jumping down off a ditch, and it had turned black and swelled up till he could hardly walk for the pain. Old Bridie Murnaghan, who had cures for most things, had put a poultice on it and told him to rest his foot till the swelling went down.

'*Rest* it?' Phil Mulligan said. 'Sure, how can I rest it? I can't afford the time!' He said the word 'rest' with a peculiar bitterness, as though it were a curse.

'You can't afford the time *not* to,' Bridie told him. 'Just be glad you've the childer to help you out around the place. You'll be off that leg for a week as it is. If you don't let it fix itself fully then you'll be off it for a month or maybe more.'

Phil Mulligan made a bad invalid. He wasn't used to inactivity. But Bridie was right about the children at least: the three boys and their mother could manage most things between them, and a week wasn't such a very long time at this time of year. It would have been different at harvest time.

As for Statia, she helped when she could – or when she was let, which wasn't the same thing. She was thirteen, and the youngest, and a girl, and her brothers seemed to take all three things as meaning she was useless. She was set to feeding poultry and doing more of the cooking – and to fetching things for her father in the house, which was the worst job because Phil Mulligan was annoyed at being laid up and seemed to be in a permanent bad humour. He'd never been sick in his life before, and he didn't like it at all. But even he knew that he was being unfair, and made rough apologies to Statia in between times.

'I hates feeling useless, child,' he'd say. 'But I shouldn't be taking it out on you.'

In some ways, though, Statia liked having her father around the house. It was a novelty. And she didn't take his bad temper to heart, because she knew it sprang mostly from worry. The boys were sensible and competent, but they hadn't their father's experience. And Phil Mulligan hated to be dependent on anyone, even his own family. Dependence was weakness in his book; and weakness frightened him.

Statia did resent the fact that she wasn't let help in the harder, outdoor work. She liked fetching cows from the fields of an evening, or any of the other things her brothers wouldn't let her do.

'Think yourself lucky, child,' her mother would advise her. 'When I was your age I was worked like a slave. We wants something better for you.'

Statia didn't understand what she meant. What could be better than knowing how to do farm work? It was all that she wanted to do. One day she hoped to be a farmer's wife herself, with a brood of boys like her mother had. What use would she be then if she'd spent her childhood being kept from learning things properly? It was very frustrating.

'I'm only a skivvy round this place,' she said to her mother. 'I'm fed up making pots of tea and throwing meal to chickens.'

'Sure, someone has to do it,' her mother pointed out. 'And you're the smallest, Statia – what do you want to do, carry bales of hay?'

Statia didn't know what to answer. But as that week passed, what with her father's foul temper and everything else, she got more and more fed up. The house and yard began to seem like a prison. She longed for a day out somewhere, away from the tea and the cleaning and the chickens. A day? An hour would do. Anything to get away from blank walls and the constant demands of her father and her brothers.

One evening towards the end of the week Statia went to open a new sack of meal to feed the hens, and found there was no new sack there. It was the kind of little thing that got overlooked in an emergency.

'It's my own fault,' Phil Mulligan admitted. 'I knew I should get some but I was putting it off. Stephen can go down to Caffertys' in the morning and ask them have they the lend of a sack till I'm back on my feet.'

But the next day there was a fresh emergency: a cow and her calf had gone straying from the boggy field near the river.

'I told youse that ditch in the bog field needed mending,' their father scowled at the boys when he heard. 'I told youse to mend that before putting any animals into the field. Now they'll end up drownded!'

And he *had* told the boys, but in their excitement at being in charge they'd forgotten. Now they all had to go and look for the strays.

'What about the feed for the hens?' Statia's mother asked.

Statia saw a chance, and took it.

'Why don't I go for it?' she asked.

'Would you be all right on your own?' her mother asked.

'Mammy!' said Statia, exasperated.

'That ass don't like hauling the cart up Mulligan's Drop,' her mother warned. 'You knows that.'

The way to Caffertys' led across the little hump-backed bridge on the Rasheen river, down in the deep river valley. On Caffertys' side the road sloped gradually up from the bridge, but on this side the land dropped suddenly down a steep hill that was known locally as Mulligan's Drop. Years ago some of Statia's ancestors – even Phil wasn't sure who, or how far back it had been – had owned the land on either side of that road: 'And 'twas a good day's work when he got out of it, whoever he was,' Phil would say, 'for 'tis useless land not worth working.'

The ass was always grand on the road to Caffertys', but sometimes gave trouble on the way back after crossing the bridge, when suddenly Mulligan's Drop became – from an ass's point of view – Mulligan's Rise.

'And why wouldn't he give trouble?' Phil Mulligan would ask sometimes. 'How would you like hauling a full cart up that hill?'

Statia had seen the way the ass, pulling the cart back along that road, would sometimes cast its broken-hearted eyes up the awful hill with a kind of shock when it reached the Rasheen bridge and – as often as not – just stand stock still in protest. When this actually happened, her father was far less understanding of its plight. Statia had often seen him break his stick uselessly on the ass's back in an effort to get it to go on.

'You'll go up there,' he'd shout at the ass, 'if I have to kick you up it! You'll go up if I have to carry you itself!'

Statia herself thought that beating only made the ass more stubborn. She'd noticed that the beast reacted better to her own soft voice and kindnesses than to her father's blows and curses. And even Phil Mulligan, reluctantly, sometimes had to admit that this was the case.

'Statia will be all right,' he said now. 'I seen her get the ass up the Drop sometimes after I'd gave up trying.'

It wasn't like him to be so supportive, and Statia guessed

he was moved by a kind of guilt for the hard time he'd been giving her. He was tempted to go with her himself, he said; he could sit in the back of the cart and still rest his ankle, and the fresh air would do him good. But Statia didn't fancy company – least of all her father's. The few hours on her own were what she wanted. And if her father came then he'd only be rushing her.

'But what if the ass won't go up the Drop for me today, Da?' she asked. 'We'd all be stuck there then.'

Her father grunted. You could see that the idea of getting out had appealed to him too. He wasn't used to staying still for such a long time.

'She's right, Phil,' Statia's mother said. 'And what if we need you here?'

'Sure, how would you need me, woman? Haven't you three big lads here? Not the cleverest lads, maybe, but they're strong.'

'No,' his wife said. 'They're not the cleverest – they takes after their father. Sure, isn't that why we needs you here to ... to *direct* them.'

Statia was surprised to see her mother giving her a wink on the sly. She hid a smile. Maybe her mother too thought her father had been hard on her this week. Maybe she too thought Statia could do with a few hours off.

Phil Mulligan was satisfied to be thought needed. He settled himself on the settle bed where he'd been all week.

'It's true for you,' he said to his wife. 'The place needs an organising brain.'

Statia could feel the muscles twitching in her cheeks. The hidden smile was trying to turn into a grin. She coughed. She wanted to get out while the going was good.

'I'll go and put the blinkers on the ass,' she said.

As Statia left the farm her mother walked a few steps of the road with her and loaded her with warnings.

'Watch out for strangers,' she said. 'If you see any men with guns then cast your eyes away from them. Don't even let on you notice them. And if you see any soldiers in lorries then be very careful. If they're Tans, get off the cart and put it between you and them, and keep your head down until they're well gone.'

There were ugly stories about drunken Tans shooting rifles at anyone they passed in their lorries. A few people had been shot and even killed. You didn't hear things like that so much about the proper police or the army, but then they tended to be sober. The problem with the Tans, people said, was that they seemed to have no discipline. The best thing to do with them was to stay out of their way altogether, but sometimes that was easier said than done.

'I won't look for you before teatime,' Statia's mother said.

'As well not to,' Statia told her. 'You know the way Mrs Cafferty loves a gossip. She'll want to know all.'

'Aye,' her mother said. 'And I knows the way Statia

Mulligan loves sitting doing nothing in the field at the butt of the Drop, too, washing her feet in the river. But you've earned a rest this week, putting up with your father. I should know – I've put up with him longer nor any of youse.'

And with a grin she turned back, not looking at Statia's flushed face. Statia felt found out. But it was true that she did love the peace and quiet in the field by the Rasheen, and that she'd sit there on her own for hours daydreaming. She even had a private place there, her only private place in all the world. It was a flat little bit of the riverbank, hidden from outside by a cluster of hazelnut trees and *sciocs* that grew in the field near the bridge. Statia had found the place several years before, chasing a new pup that hadn't yet learned to come when she called. She'd seen him disappear into the bushes and, never thinking, had pushed through after him. She'd expected to hear a splash as the pup fell in the water, and was already hoping she wouldn't have to go in after him. The Rasheen wasn't deep or dangerous, but she didn't fancy getting her clothes wet because of any stupid dog. But there had been no splash, and to her surprise she'd found the pup, his tail wagging and his tongue lolling, sitting on a little flat bit of the bank between the nut trees and the water. It was a sunny little nook hedged in by the scraping branches of the low trees, invisible except from the other side of the river, hardly noticeable even from there: a couple of square feet of grass hidden from the world.

It had been a sunny day, like today, and when she'd sat beside the dog – there was just about room for her, even then – she'd found she was at exactly the right height to dangle her bare feet in the cool water. The pup had pressed against her, his tongue lolling, looking up into her face. Statia had almost imagined he looked proud.

See the fine place that I found for you, she'd imagined him saying. Aren't I a grand dog?

And she'd almost replied to his imagined question, and reassured him that he was. The little place – its peace, its privacy – had enchanted her from the start. When she was younger, and had less work to keep her busy, she'd often gone there. Nowadays – even before this week – she seldom found the time. As soon as she heard of the need for someone to go to Caffertys' she pictured the river as it must be today, sparkling and rippling in the hot sun, gurgling cool over the stones below the little bridge. She imagined the trout rising, leaving ripples on the spangled water. The idea of sitting there for half an hour, in her secret, private spot, with the sun shining down and her feet trailing in the water, and no-one looking for anything off her, or bossing her, had filled her with a sudden hungry yearning. She should have known her Ma would see it on her face – her Ma could read her like a book.

There was no need to be embarrassed, she told herself. Hadn't Ma said she understood? She even approved. It was a rare thing to do something nice that your Ma approved of. Statia felt suddenly free. She took a deep breath and relaxed. The day was hers. The house, with its stormy man and big bostoons of brothers, could look after itself for the afternoon.

It was a lovely day. The birds sang in the roadside hedges. The air was alive with the buzzing of bees and flies. The ass clopped along the road at his own pace, and Statia lost herself in dreams. After a while she came to the lip of Mulligan's Drop and started down the steep hill. It was very quiet, and over the roll of the wheels and the clop of the ass's hooves you could hear the water of the Rasheen clucking in its stony bed. The ass dug in his heels against the slope, no longer pulling the cart but pressing back against it as he descended the straight road. Statia got down and took hold of his harness, speaking softly to him and yanking back when he seemed about to give in to the weight of the cart and pull forward.

'Come on now, *a mhic*,' she said mildly. 'We're nearly down. You're doing grand. Good lad!'

The ass's ears twitched at her soft tones. He shivered with the strain. At least he wouldn't try and stop here, with the weight pressing him on.

At the foot of the Drop the road levelled out before climbing very slightly for maybe ten yards towards the hump-backed stone bridge. The water in the river chuckled and gurgled, inviting her to dawdle. But Statia got back up on the cart and went on, humming to herself. She'd seen nobody since leaving home except for one old man driving a few dozy-looking cattle. He'd saluted her briefly, raising the switch in his hand to the peak of his tattered cap. Statia had greeted him in return. She didn't recognise him, but she knew that men like this weren't what her mother meant by 'strangers'. This was only a farmer like themselves.

*　　*　　*

At Caffertys' Statia was welcomed. Simon Cafferty had bought three sacks of hen-meal only the week before.

'I usually only buys the two,' he said, 'but I got a good price on these, and I knew the extra one wouldn't go astray.'

He was glad to lend one to the Mulligans, and Statia had to assure him that one would be enough. Simon even loaded the sack in the cart for her while Statia was given tea and bread and butter and had a chat with his wife in Caffertys' kitchen.

'I'll call up when I get the time,' Simon said to Statia when she was leaving, 'and see if I can do anything for youse. And if there's anything in the meantime, youse have only to let me know.'

Then he leaned forward and, looking up into Statia's face, said in a lower voice: 'There was an Auxie patrol out on the roads this morning. If you see them coming ...'

'I know, I know,' Statia said. 'Me Mammy have me warned about them.'

'And so she should,' Simon Cafferty said. 'You wouldn't

be the first person they left dead on the roads behind them. They're worse nor the Tans, them fellows.' And he spat on the ground in disgust at the thought of the foreigners.

Statia set out on the road home, glad to have the business end of things over with. By the time she got back her brothers would have started mooching around the house, wondering when their tea would be ready.

'Oh well,' she said to the ass, 'we had a bit of a day out anyhow. And the best bit is to come.'

She'd decided from the first to save her visit to the river for the return journey. She'd been tempted, on the way, by the cool-looking water clucking over the smooth stones, but she'd known that the business of the corn would weigh on her mind. Now, with the sack safe in the bed of the cart, she could relax. It would give the ass a rest, too, before the long haul up the Drop. That would make it all the easier to persuade him up. As the summer sun beat down, Statia found herself nearly dozing on the cart. Once when she'd sat with her feet in the Rasheen – on a day much like this one, come to think of it – a trout had come and nibbled curiously at her toes. The river was sniving with them at this time of year. Maybe it would happen again today. Her brothers, if something like that happened, would have tried to catch the fish; but Statia wouldn't dream of doing that, even though she loved a bit of fried trout. She'd often watched the fish stirring dreamily in the Rasheen, darting along or staying still with just the odd flip of their tails.

She'd envied them sometimes, with all day to dream. She could dream for a while herself, now.

She was coming up to the hump-backed bridge again when, above the rushing noise of the water, she heard the sound of approaching motors. She looked up towards the lip of Mulligan's Drop. The cab of a lorry appeared over the brow of the hill. Then the rest of the lorry came into view, looming from a great cloud of dust. It was a police tender, the back full of Auxiliaries. There was a Lewis gun mounted on the top of the cab, and an Auxie stood behind it with the ribbons of his Glengarry cap fluttering.

The tender came down the slope towards her, followed by another. They were both full of armed men. Statia's heart dropped even quicker than the lorries coming down the hill. She felt a cold fear in her belly at the sight of the dark, dusty uniforms. *Don't look at them*, she told herself. *Get down off the cart this minute and don't even look at them.* But it was hard to tear her eyes away from the lorries. They bristled with gunbarrels, dark and dangerous. They were like big hunting animals completely out of place in this quiet countryside. And when Statia did finally look away, staring towards the river for some familiar, comforting sight, she was shocked to see there a man she didn't know. He was standing up over his knees in the waters of the Rasheen near the bridge, and he was waving at her frantically. Statia, taken by surprise, stared at him. She frowned. The man waved both arms at her, as though hooshing her back the way she'd come. What was he at? She –

The whole world dissolved in a big bang and a flash like the end of time. Statia was sure that she screamed, but she could hear nothing. She was flung, stunned, from the cart. She lay on her back in the dust of the road, dazed and blinking. When she looked around she could see hardly anything. It was as though she was in the middle of a cloud.

I'm blinded! she thought. *Blinded altogether!*

But she wasn't blinded. She really was in a cloud. The cloud was made of dust, she realised, as it thinned and settled. Dust and smoke. She could see the donkey now, still between the shafts of the cart but lying stretched out on the road with his mild eyes closed and his great head between his outflung forelegs. His back legs had buckled under him, and his rump was in the air. He looked like he was bowing down to the sight before him. And when Statia looked, that sight was surely strange enough to bow down to. There was a shimmering twinkle of lights from the Auxie tenders, which had come to a halt ahead of her, across the bridge. And the bridge ...

Statia shook her head to clear it. There was a ringing in her ears, but no other sound. She stared ahead. The bridge over the Rasheen ... she squinted at it, unsure of what she was seeing. The bridge hadn't entirely disappeared, but a great ragged chunk of it was simply *gone*.

A mine, she told herself. *They mined the bridge!*

She said this to herself almost calmly, but she was more

dazed than calm. She couldn't quite believe that any of this was real. Everything seemed to be happening very slowly, and in complete silence. She remembered the man in the river. She turned her head to look to where she'd seen him. The man was still there, but there were two other men standing with him now. They climbed up on the bank and were scrambling onto the roadway ahead of her. They were carrying rifles. As Statia watched, they lay down flat in the roadbed, sheltered by the amputated stump of the hump-backed bridge, and started firing their rifles towards the Auxiliary tenders. One of them – the man who'd been waving at her – turned and waved again. There was no mistaking his message this time: he was telling her to go away.

All of this took place in a world that for Statia was absolutely silent except for the ringing in her ears. She could still see the tenders, trapped between the blown bridge and the steep hill behind them. The rear one was still on the slope. The twinkle of lights that she'd seen still went on, and she realised finally that the lights were gunflashes. As she watched, the Auxies abandoned their tenders. They jumped out and lay in the road. But some of them stayed in the tenders. Those would be the dead. Statia looked back up at Mulligan's Drop. From the top of it she saw more flashes coming from the hedges and bushes. And still all was silent.

Statia tried to guess how many Auxies had been in the

tenders, but she couldn't. That they were in a very bad position, whatever their numbers, even she could see that. The foremost tender was only a few yards from the wrecked bridge. Its cab was burnt out and smoking, caught full-on by the explosion of the mine. The windscreen was gone, and a dark, burnt, motionless figure slumped over what was left of the steering wheel. The Auxies on the road were exposed to a raking fire from the high ground above them, and when Statia looked she saw more gunflashes coming from this side of the river.

She was still sitting beside the cart. There wasn't a stir out of the ass: he was either insensible or dead. His fall had dragged the cartshafts down till their front ends were on the ground, so that the back of the cart itself stood raised to the sky. Statia put a hand out and rested it on the cart, to push herself up. Something smacked into the wood a couple of inches from her fingers. She stared, puzzled. It happened again, even closer to her hand this time. A big splinter of wood flew from the cart, raking the back of her hand in its passing. Blood welled in the long, shallow scrape. Suddenly understanding, Statia jerked her hand off the wood as though from a hot pan. Those were bullets that were hitting the cart. Statia scrambled round the back of the near wheel and into the shelter of the cart's raised body. She curled into a ball and closed her eyes and listened to the ringing in her ears, suddenly glad of her deafness.

She'd no idea, afterwards, of how long she lay there. It

felt like forever, but it could have been no more than a few minutes. Gradually her hearing came back. She heard the storm of gunfire and the cries of shot men. She heard curses roared. The sounds were all mixed up with the endless clucking sound of the river, that sound which had always seemed peaceful to her before. More explosions came – grenades or bombs, she guessed – and more screams. One scream in particular went on and on, like the sound of the river itself. It was an endless wail that spoke of an agony Statia didn't even want to think about. Anybody feeling such pain should be dead – they'd be better off dead. But the wail just went on, rising and falling, endlessly.

They were feared men, the Auxies, and hated – more feared and hated than the Tans in a way, precisely because they had the discipline the Tans lacked. There was more cold cruelty in their acts, and more thought. But now as she listened to their cries Statia heard only the sound of the pain, and she wanted it only to stop. She covered her ears with her hands and she lay there, shivering, wanting to scream herself.

Go away! she thought. *Go away, all of you, this minute!*

They didn't go away. The intensity of the gunfire, though, did begin to lessen. Statia started to believe that it might even end. She didn't care who won, so long as it all stopped. But then there was a new sound, a sound she didn't notice at first over the diminished shooting. It was the sound of another motor. Suddenly the firing grew to a fresh crescendo. A machinegun opened up, and there were repeated volleys of rifle fire. Bullets smacked off the ground around the cart, and off the cart itself. Statia heard a strange, animal whimpering. It came from very close by. For a moment she thought that it must be the ass; but she'd noticed a pool of blood growing around the still figure of the poor brute between the shafts, and she knew that the ass was dead. She realised that the sound was coming from herself. She tried to stop it, but she couldn't. Her mouth had become like a stranger's, beyond her control.

Running footsteps approached. Statia saw several sets of flying feet go by. One set stumbled, and a man fell full length on the road with his face only a couple of feet from her own, staring at her from wide-open eyes. His mouth was open too. He had long yellow teeth, and several of them were missing. With his wide eyes and his open mouth, he seemed almost to be laughing. But there was no life in his eyes, and she realised he was dead. He wasn't an Auxie. His cap lay in the roadway, and the rifle that had dropped from his hand. Someone came and picked up the rifle, then ran on. The dead man lay grinning at Statia, like someone who'd been frozen in the act of playing 'peep' with her.

Peep! said the dead man's grin. *I sees you there.*

Statia stared at the man's face for a very long moment, at the wide, staring eyes, dead and cold, like a fish staring back at her. Then she shrieked and scrabbled out from under the cart. She crouched there like an animal on the open road, whimpering, then risked a look up towards the scene of the ambush.

At the brow of Mulligan's Drop she saw the cab of another Auxiliary tender. A Lewis gun on its roof was sending burst after burst of machinegun fire into the hedges lining the roadway down the Drop, and into the fields on either side. Lumps were flying off the hedges, and puffs of dirt spitting out of the ground. Dark-uniformed men were already in the fields, shouting and shooting. At the foot of the hill, the surviving Auxies from the first two tenders had regrouped. Some of them, she saw, were making for the river, to ford it. There was no sign of any answering gunfire. The attackers had cut and run: they'd been taken by surprise, and ambushed in their turn. A few of them lay dead or wounded in the field and on the road. She saw an Auxie with a pistol standing over one wounded man. As Statia watched, the Auxie reached out the pistol carefully and shot the man in the head.

Statia stared goggle-eyed at the scene across the bridge. The hedges were blackened and burning, the very road stained with blood and oil and black, twisted wreckage from the burning tenders. There were no birds singing now. She realised that the wailing man, whether ambusher or Auxie, had stopped his noise – dead now, no doubt, and probably glad of it. The ambush was over: her wish had come true.

Then a bullet tore a great gouge in the side of the cart

near her face. She saw it happen even before she heard the shot. When she looked she saw the Auxie who'd fired. He was standing in the middle of the river, in almost the same spot where she'd first seen the ambusher only a little while before. The Auxie was still pointing his rifle at her, and she saw several others raise their weapons too. This was not a wild shot, she realised: the man had quite deliberately fired at her. He had meant for her, Statia, to die.

They're going to kill me, she thought. *They think I was in on it, and they're going to kill me.*

It was the last straw. Her brain froze. Her stomach clenched. Pure animal fear drove her scrambling across the road and over the ditch. None of the Auxies had reached this bank of the river yet. They were moving carefully, wary of ambushers who might still lie in wait. Statia didn't move warily at all. She fled pell mell over ditches and stiles, through stands of trees and thorny hedges, down narrow, twisting, half-overgrown lanes between fields. She had no plan beyond putting as much distance as possible between herself and the ambush scene, and even to say that she planned that was wrong: she fled as any other animal might, the last vestiges of her sense cracked by the thought that these frightening men meant to take her life.

Later she didn't know how long she'd run for. It might have been five minutes or an hour. She fled through the empty land, falling and getting back up, running and scrabbling and pushing herself on. Sometimes she went on her hands and knees. She couldn't have stopped if she'd wanted to; and she didn't want to stop. She wasn't a child now; in her blank terror she was hardly even human: she was an animal fleeing its death. She could not have fled more desperately if there'd been a devil behind her, snapping at her ankles, keen to tear out her heart and her soul. In the end she stopped when she fell for the twentieth time, and this time couldn't get up any more. She lay gasping in great shuddering breaths, pain like a hatchet ripping through her ribs and lungs and chest with every breath she took. Then she passed out.

*   *   *

When she woke up she lay looking at the sky, wondering where and who and what she was. It came back to her like a slap in the face, the memories of screams and shots, the burning tenders and the charred hump of the Auxie driver slumped over the steering wheel in the burned-out cab. She lay shivering in her whole body for a time. Then she caught hold of herself and made herself sit up. She was in a field on a green hill, just inside an open wooden gate. She knew at once where she was, recognising it from a fairy rath by the hedge as one of Caffertys' outlying fields. She was at least three miles from Mulligan's Drop, nowhere near home.

She drew her knees up and buried her face in her skirt. The skirt was ripped and tattered from thorns and hedges she'd burst through, not noticing. Her arms and legs were bleeding from a hundred little cuts. She clasped the torn arms around the bruised knees and huddled there, shaking. She felt very small in the big world around her. After a long time she made herself stand. She looked around. She saw no-one. The world was silent again except for the birds and the bees and, somewhere, the distant sound of a single motor. She was back in the still, country world that she'd been in before the ambush – her own world. It was hard to believe the assault had happened at all. But she was still shivering, and still bleeding, and she knew that the ambush had happened, all right. It was this world now, this world she had known all her life, that seemed almost a dream.

She'd get nowhere, she knew, standing here like this. She had to go somewhere, to find people. She remembered the cold eyes of the Auxies as they'd focused on her, and the one standing in the waters of the Rasheen who'd actually shot at her. She'd glimpsed something in those cold eyes more terrible than anything else she'd seen in that place, more frightening than the bodies and the burning. She'd seen death there: her death. Auxies were always wild after an ambush – who wouldn't be? They went mad for revenge, and they often burned houses near an ambush site – burned houses, and beat or killed people they thought must have known about the attack or even people who couldn't have known about it. And they'd thought Statia was involved. They'd meant to kill her – she'd seen it in those awful eyes. They might still shoot her if they found her. They might shoot her dead.

She could go to Caffertys', she supposed. But the Auxies might be there already, drunk with vengeful madness. Another cold pang stabbed Statia's gut at the thought. The day was declining now, the sun lower in the sky. There was a first faint breath of coolness in the air. From where the sun stood, Statia guessed she'd been unconscious for maybe two hours. That would have been plenty of time for the Auxies to reach Caffertys' roadside home. But then, with a rush of relief, she realised that was impossible: the great hole blown in the Rasheen bridge would make it impassable for the tenders, and the Auxies would have gone nowhere on foot – they might have walked straight into another ambush. Any detour they made, on the other hand, would have taken them well out of the area: the bridge at the Drop was the only one over the Rasheen for miles. And the Auxies were in no state to go looking for revenge anyway. If they'd gone anywhere then they'd have gone back to their barracks, to have their wounded tended. They'd drink, and they'd rage, and when darkness fell they'd darken their faces and they'd pick up their guns and they'd get in other tenders … and then they'd go burning. And it wasn't dark yet. No, the Auxies had certainly just gone back the way they came, as quickly as they could.

For one small minute she nearly relaxed, but then, as another thought struck her, the coldness in Statia's stomach came again. It wasn't a stab of cold this time, but a slow, spreading thing like a wave, and it spread till it chilled

happened, she didn't need to go the full five miles. She smelled the burning from a long way off, and when she raised up her eyes she saw the thickening column of smoke climbing into the darkening sky. She stopped and stared, knowing what was burning; then, slowly and determinedly now, she began to walk towards the fires.

The King of Irishtown

'I'm blue in the face talking to him,' my mother said. 'It does no good at all. That child is just wilful.'

'Of course he is,' my father said. 'Every child is wilful. It's part of being young.'

It was me they were discussing, or rather my many failings. My mother, as usual, was giving out about me, while my father tried to defend me without actually contradicting her. My father was an easygoing man, a man who valued peace above all else; and in our house that meant making a lot of compromises, because my mother was a woman who had very set opinions on a great number of things. I was in the hall, listening, though I don't know why I bothered: these conversations always went the same way. My mother would go on about how I was Letting Her Down ('though it's yourself you're letting down, if you only knew it,' she'd tell me. 'You'll realise that one day, when it's too late to repair your good name.'). My father, while indulging her as best he could, would try to defend me from her worst accusations.

'I won't have him answering back like that,' my mother said. 'It's disgraceful.'

'Oh it is,' said my father. 'Totally disgraceful. Still, he owned up straight away. And he does stick by his pals – I like that in a fellow.'

'That depends,' said my mother icily, 'who a fellow's *pals* are.'

She made the word 'pals' sound like something dirty – as in my case, to my mother, it was. This was what lay at the root of the trouble between us. What my mother disapproved of so strongly wasn't so much the things that I did, it was the people that I did them with. When Phil Murphy, the police sergeant, had brought me home earlier that day and told her I'd been playing with a gang that kicked a football through a window, my mother hadn't even asked him who the other boys were. She hadn't needed to: she'd known.

'A football?' she said to Phil Murphy. 'A bundle of rags wrapped around a stone, you mean. That lot wouldn't have a football unless they robbed one somewhere.'

Phil Murphy nodded his great red head in agreement.

'And if they did rob one itself,' he said, 'it wouldn't be the first time. It's terrible to see such a respectable young boy ruining himself in such company.'

That was the real root of the problem – respectability. We lived in a market town in the midlands, where my father owned and ran the local newspaper. That wasn't as grand as it might sound – there were only a few people working on the paper, and my father did most of the writing and even some of the printing. Still, it was *the newspaper,* and that meant we were a highly respectable family by the standards of that most respectable town. Being respectable, to my mother, was terribly important. As a *respectable* boy, I should have mixed with other respectable boys – boys like Eddie Gregg, the pale, lisping doctor's son, or the insufferably smug Byrnes of the Shannon Vale Hotel, or any one of a dozen tedious merchants' or publicans' sons. But I was drawn to boys who *weren't* respectable – who were, in fact, anything *but* respectable. And that was something my mother could neither stand nor understand.

But 'respectable', to me, was another word for boring, and what I liked in a friend were things I never found in the boys she'd have liked me to mix with. I liked boys who were funny, and daring, and lively, and loyal; I liked friends who had a bit of go in them. I found none of these virtues in the boys that my mother favoured. As for the friends that I did have, I was drawn to them mainly because they seemed to me to have all of these qualities in abundance. But as well as that they seemed to have far more interesting lives than I did – in fact, I was downright jealous of their lives. They had freedom, and they had big families that squabbled and fought and made up their quarrels and laughed and cried together in their cramped, lively homes. I, on the other hand, was an only child. Our home was anything but lively.

We never laughed out loud together as a family, or even had a proper row. Those, my mother thought, were uncouth things to do. We were far too respectable for such common behaviour. In our house you could go for hours without hearing any sound beyond the clock ticking, or my mother complaining about the latest maid. In my friends' houses, where I was accepted without question, I felt I could share a little bit in a bigger sort of life, a common life that, without really knowing it, I suppose I longed to be a part of.

All my friends, do you see, came from the rundown part of the town called Irishtown, where the poor people lived. Irishtown, so far as my mother was concerned, was a sort of moral leper colony. She wouldn't even hire a servant from there, she said. Between their dirt and their thieving, you wouldn't know what to sack them for.

'Irishtown' always struck me as a funny name: we were all Irish in the town, after all – even the respectable folk. I asked my father about the name one time and he said he supposed there was an Irishtown or Irish Street in every town in Ireland. They were leftover names from the old times, he said, when the Irish weren't let live in the town proper. This only raised fresh questions in my mind. Who *had* lived in the town then, I wanted to know, and what had become of them? And why hadn't the Irish been let live in the town proper? This was Ireland, after all: this was their country.

But my father only made a certain face and waved me away.

I suspected, from the face my father made when I asked about it, that the story of Irishtown had something to do with politics. My father had a particular disgusted look that he always got on his face when that subject came up. He had to cover political events in the paper, but that didn't mean he liked doing it. Our country, he often said, had had too much politics: too much politics and too much fighting. For some people it amounted to the same thing. Only a couple of years before there'd been an insurrection in Dublin, when a handful of lunatics had tried to seize the city and declare the country independent – without so much as a by your leave (my mother said) to the people whose 'freedom' they said they were fighting for. The army had mopped them up in a week, but a lot of people had been killed and – worse – a lot of property damaged. The upstart rebels had shamed the name of Ireland, my mother said. It was bad enough, she said, having the big war going on in France, draining the life's blood of Europe; at least – until 1916 – we'd been spared the horror of warfare on our doorstep. But some people wouldn't be satisfied till they had their own homes burning around them, and their neighbours' too – especially their neighbours'. Some people were just spiteful like that, she said. It was pure envy.

Most of the other respectable people of the town shared my mother's view of these things, though I'd noticed that a lot of the Irishtown folk admired the 1916 rebels. Some of them hung pictures of the rebels' executed leaders in their houses, cheap prints torn from penny papers and tacked up on the plastered clay walls. I'd asked my father about that, but he'd just said that the poor could afford to favour revolutions – they'd less to lose. And he'd warned me, for the hundredth time, never to let my mother know that I actually went inside my friends' houses in Irishtown, because she'd worry about dirt and consumption and lice.

'You know your mother,' he said. 'She gets worried when she has nothing to worry about.'

And she worried endlessly about my friends. They were guilty of the greatest crime she knew: being poor. And that annoyed me. My Irishtown friends were honest, by their own lights, and by anyone's standards they were adventurous. They were also reliable – true blue, as we said then. They were my pals, so I stuck with them, to my mother's despair.

'It's you he gets that off,' I heard her say in a moment of anger to my father once. 'You that would talk to any dog in the street.'

Needless to say, we had no dog ourselves: my mother said they were dirty brutes, and would destroy the house. All of my Irishtown friends had dogs, of course, and their dogs had the freedom of their houses and ate the same food as the family – what there was of it. These dogs were mostly mongrel terriers, each with more character, on average, than most of my mother's human friends put together. We'd often bring them, in packs, to hunt rabbits – the dogs, I mean – in the fields around the town, or rats in the cramped backyards of Irishtown that backed onto the river. It was great sport, but it was more than sport to my friends: the rabbits were a welcome addition to their households' larders, while every dead rat was a cause for celebration in those infested shanties. Many's the baby in Irishtown whose toes would have been nibbled by rats if it hadn't been for those terriers. Irishtowners loathed rats; they loathed them even more than they loathed policemen. I don't know that the rats had any particular feelings about the Irishtowners; in the case of the police, though, the loathing was mutual.

* * *

Phil Murphy, the sergeant who'd brought me home after the window-breaking, was the special enemy of Irishtowners. It wouldn't be stretching things at all to say that he hated them, and blamed them for every crime that happened in our town. They hated him, too; but more importantly to Phil Murphy, they feared him. He liked to boast of how the tough men of Irishtown were more fearful of him than of any other man, and he called himself, when the mood was on him, the King of Irishtown.

'They may have their pictures of rebels,' he'd say, 'and talk all they like of republics. But there's one king they'll never get rid of in Irishtown, and that's Phil Murphy.'

Phil Murphy would quite happily have razed Irishtown to the ground, as I heard him say himself on more than one occasion: razed it to the ground with the people still in it, even the women and children. Since he wasn't allowed to do that, he was content to be its king – and a true tyrant he was.

There were eight policemen in the barracks in our town, and Phil Murphy was in charge of them. He was a giant of a man, even among all those tall policeman. They were generally amiable men, the Royal Irish Constabulary, at least in my experience of them. But Phil Murphy was different. He was a former police boxing champion, and I always sensed an air of violence off him that set him apart from other RIC men. I could feel his eye on me down the length of a whole street, and it was rarely my imagination when I did feel it. He took a special interest in me – for my poor parents' sake, he said. I need hardly tell you that it wasn't an interest I welcomed.

My mother would always make tea for Phil Murphy when he called, as he did once a week or so, for a social visit. She'd serve it in the best china at the good table in the parlour, and give him a big plate of lardy cake to go with it. Phil Murphy loved my mother's lardy cake. Crumbs of it would stick to his moustache as he ate, and every now and then he'd lick them off with a flick of his thick red tongue. He was really a huge man, very tall and bulky, with red face and hair and a big, drooping red moustache that hung over his top lip like a fringe. His neck was red too, thick and fat and red. In our parlour he'd carefully take off his cork-lined helmet and put it daintily down among the tea things on the table. From the collar up then he was red, and from the collar down he was the dark bottle green of his uniform. He and my mother would discuss me over the tea, while I sat sullenly listening and pretending not to. Sometimes I'd glance up slyly, but Phil Murphy's cool blue eyes would always catch me.

They always talked about me as though I wasn't there.

'You'd think he'd have more sense all the same,' Phil Murphy would say to my mother. 'Sure, there's not one of them boyos that hasn't had kin in trouble – brothers and fathers and, aye, probably grandfathers. And the women are no better. They're a bad lot up there in Irishtown, ma'am. Criminality runs in their very blood.'

'I've tried everything,' my mother would confess in despair. 'Even beating him does no good.'

'I suppose at their age, now, it's mostly harmless enough,' Phil Murphy would say. 'But it will be very different in a couple of years. What's play in a child isn't always so playful in a young man. What's play for a child can land a young man in the law-courts. And it wouldn't be a nice thing for his father to have to write about his own son in the court reports in your own paper. And then, of course, you'd wonder even now what some people would be thinking, seeing such a respectable child running wild with the dregs of the town.'

He had, I knew, put his finger on the core of my mother's problem. In the end her worries had nothing to do with me at all. What really worried her was how my doings might reflect on her, and on her social standing: what would the other 'decent' people think of her, letting me loose in the streets with the despised ones? By 'decent' people my mother meant the merchant and professional classes of the town – the sort of people she came from. Most of them, like herself, were the descendants of people who'd run the same businesses before them, a little clutch of families who'd controlled the town since the last century. Such people viewed the residents of Irishtown with an open hostility made up of suspicion, dislike and contempt. In their hearts I suspected they viewed everyone like that, but in the case of Irishtowners they took no trouble to hide it. I knew that these merchants – all pillars of society, pillars of the Church, pillars of the local councils and societies for the improvement of this and that, and notorious, some of them, for their slyness and penny-pinching, their deceit and their greed, some even owning the rundown hovels where my friends were forced to live – viewed my friends and all belonging to them as the scum of the earth. I got angry whenever I thought about that, so I thought of it as little as I could. My loyalty to my friends got me in enough trouble; I dreaded to think how my mother might react if she ever found out what I really felt about the 'decent' people whose good opinion she so fretted over.

Phil Murphy would linger on these occasions of tea and cake. In theory he had duties to perform, but they could always wait. He had a good life as the police sergeant in our town. The police had it easy there. Even the cattle-driving that still plagued some other parts of the Midlands was uncommon. Nothing much happened by way of great excitement. On fairdays there'd be fights as the pubs closed, and now and again someone would thieve something or be caught poaching, or there'd be some dispute over land or cattle, or various sorts of petty theft; but these things happened everywhere. They were so ordinary that it would have been far stranger if they hadn't happened at all.

Much of such crime as there was in the town was – quite rightly – put down to the Irishtowners. They fought among themselves, the Irishtowners, and of course they thieved, though they were often caught. And they poached, though they were less often caught there. With both the theft and poaching, it was pretty much a case of steal or go hungry: none of them had much money, and hunger was an everyday thing in most of their houses. Many of the men had joined the British army for the wages, and more than a few of them had died in the war. The sons of the local gentry too had enlisted in the army during the war – those that hadn't army careers already – but I'd noticed that very few from the more respectable classes of the town had joined up. Loudly law-abiding and respectable though they all were, these had supported the anti-conscription movement when the British had threatened to extend army conscription to Ireland. In some places, earlier that year, anti-conscription protesters had clashed with the police, but naturally this hadn't happened in our town. There the anti-conscription campaign had been very civilised – very respectable. There'd been big public meetings where stirring speeches were made about how Irishmen could not be forced to go and fight for a foreign power. Often these speeches were made by some of the prominent merchants who were thriving on the high wartime prices but who didn't want their own sons and heirs going off to fight. Shocking treasons were preached at these meetings sometimes, in the heat of the moment. I remember Tom D'Arcy, the publican and town councillor, saying how Irishmen would fight conscription with their bare hands if they had to; how they'd fight for the right not to fight, and die for the right not to die. I'd been at that meeting with some of the Irishtown lads, and we tried to puzzle out Tom D'Arcy's meaning.

'Sure it's only ould tosh,' Mickey Farrell said. 'It's his own sons he's worried about. He begrudges the money he'd have to pay someone to help in the shop if they died.'

Mickey was only eleven, but a cynical attitude came naturally to Irishtowners. If they weren't born with it, the world soon taught it to them. But what he said started me thinking.

*　　*　　*

The other incident that started me thinking about the way our whole town was run, was the homecoming of Mickey Farrell's big brother, Tom. That summer, unnoticed by any but his Irishtown neighbours and his family, Tom Farrell came home from jail in England. He'd been working in Dublin for years, and he'd been out fighting with the rebels there in the Rising. He'd survived the fighting, and after the surrender he'd been sent to prison. The whole of Irishtown was keen to see him when he came back, and I was as keen as any of them. There were plenty of people in Irishtown who'd been arrested for one little thing or another, but I'd never seen anyone who'd been in jail for armed rebellion and treason before. My own small rebellions seemed puny when put against his.

Tom Farrell was a small, wiry, handsome man, and I suppose he'd have been about twenty-one the first time I saw him. I was disappointed in him at first, to tell you the truth. I'd expected someone more dangerous-looking, more bitter – someone altogether more exciting. But Tom just seemed a friendly young man – a gas character, full of jokes and songs and funny stories about his time in jail. I quickly got over my disappointment, and hung on his every word. It isn't every day you meet a man who's taken up arms against a whole empire, and it was a far rarer thing in 1918 than it would be even a couple of years later.

I first saw Tom on the afternoon of his return. His family and neighbours had gathered some money somewhere and laid in jugs of ale and porter and a little keg of whiskey they'd got from one of the Irishtown shebeens. They'd bought and cooked dozens of pigs' feet and cheeks and what looked like half a hundredweight of ribs. They'd boiled a barrowload of potatoes, and there were rounds of brown bread the size of the wheels on a dogcart, and a big yellow brick of butter. There was more money spent on food and drink that day than the family would normally spend in several months, and no doubt some of the stuff was robbed somewhere (tasting, as Tom himself said, all the better for it). But it wasn't every day, as old Granny Farrell commented, that you got a young fellow home that was after dying for Ireland. The neighbours crowded the already-crowded house, and there was music and dancing and singing and laughing. Dogs and children rolled on the floor, and as the day progressed and the drink did its work they were joined, sometimes unintentionally, by a few of the revellers. It was a great day entirely, and when it was time for me to go home for my tea I left late, grudgingly, dragging myself away, hating the fact that I had to go at all. I had no interest in eating. I was stuffed with fatty bacon and brown bread anyway, and stuffed in a different way with the talk and the laughter and the singing. I walked home to my silent, respectable house, hating every step.

I heard afterwards that later that night Tom went out with a few of his friends to continue the celebration. On his way home alone, merry if not downright drunk, he discovered that someone outside of Irishtown had noticed his return after all: Phil Murphy and two of his constables waylaid him, and while the constables held Tom's arms the where respectable people didn't care to go. Not all of the constables took part in these special actions, and some of them – for there were many decent men in the RIC, no matter what anyone says – certainly disapproved. But Murphy was the boss, and he was a bully with it.

My mother was furious when I mentioned the incident at home – an unwise thing to do, but my anger got the better of me – and she threatened to wash my mouth out with soap.

'That's pure Irishtown lies,' she said. 'I won't have you repeating them here. Sergeant Murphy would never do anything like that. It was probably a drunken fight Farrell was in, with some of his own low companions. A jailbird like that slandering good policemen! He should be put back in jail where he belongs!'

When I said to my father that he should report the assault in the newspaper, he smiled at me sadly.

'It's not news, son,' he said.

'Not news? But he'd done nothing. The police attacked him! It's an injustice!'

My father sighed.

'Son,' he said, 'it's not the business of the police to enforce justice. It's the business of the police to enforce the law and to keep order. Phil Murphy was keeping order in his own way. I may think it's unjust, but who am I?'

'You're the newspaper owner – people should be told about this!'

My father sighed again. He looked at me as though wondering whether I'd come down in the last shower.

'And who in this town,' he asked me, 'do you think will want to read about police handing out a beating to a rebel from Irishtown?'

*   *   *

The British army's need for fresh troops faded as 1918 wore on. The German war effort collapsed, and in November we had the Armistice and the Great War finally ended. There was little sense of victory in our town. People had got used to war, as they get used to anything. But there was more to it than that. People grew uneasy. Farmers and merchants – the very merchants who'd played a big part in the campaign against conscription – grumbled as they foresaw the end of their profits from high wartime prices. Even those Irish-towners depending on army wages wondered what would become of them when their husbands or fathers or sons were demobilised. These would no longer be brave soldiers fighting the enemy; instead they'd be unemployed men, used to violence, wandering the streets of a town that had no use for them.

'This is when we need our politicians in parliament, to work for us,' Phil Murphy said to my father. 'And there they are off sulking.'

The Irish Parliamentary Party had withdrawn in protest from the London Parliament in April, when the Conscription Bill was forced through.

'It will all be different after the election,' my father said to Phil Murphy. 'We'll know where we are then.'

The general election called for December that year marked the point where politics finally came to our town in a big way. It was the first election held under new rules which let far more people vote. To the astonishment and disgust of many, even Irishtowners would have votes, and the novelty alone caused much excitement there. The town was even to have a candidate from the rebel party, Sinn Féin, the ones who'd been involved in the Dublin rebellion. Nothing like this had happened in our town before. The area had returned the same Member of Parliament for over twenty years, a prosperous farmer called Jonty Lehane who supported the Parliamentary Party and was an old friend of the party leader, John Redmond. He was a popular speaker with a great fondness for port, good brandy and the sound of his own voice. My father, who'd seen him speak in public many times, said Mr Lehane was a true moderate, for he'd never seen him either altogether sober or altogether drunk. My mother told my father he should be ashamed of himself – Mister Lehane's cousin, she said, was a bishop. Mister Lehane himself had a speech impediment, she said, and it sometimes made him slur his words. But even my father, mild man though he was, couldn't brook such nonsense.

'A speech impediment?' he said almost bitterly. 'Aye – a cork from a brandy bottle got stuck in his gullet, maybe.'

My mother just sniffed, in the way that she had, as though what he said wasn't worth responding to.

I'd noticed a growing tendency in my father that summer to contradict my mother, in small things at least. It was always hard to know my father's true feelings about serious things, because he always liked to be agreeable where possible. But I thought I could feel a difference in him, an impatience with the people my mother so admired, and whose meaningless respect and approval she craved.

Naturally, my Irishtown friends and I were all mad supporters of Sinn Féin. None of us was certain what the party stood for, except that it stood for change. But that was more than enough. We saw how the Sinn Féiners – the Shinners, people called them – made the respectable people nervous, and for me that alone seemed proof of their worth. Still, when the first posters for the Sinn Féin candidate appeared – in Irishtown, of course – I was genuinely astonished, because the candidate named on the posters was none other than Tom Farrell. I hadn't heard a word about this beforehand. When I asked Mickey, he said he was as surprised as I was.

'We had a few strangers called to the house, all right,' he said. 'And they'd go into corners and whisper about stuff with Tom. But I thought it was just about ordinary stuff – thieving things and that.'

Phil Murphy was keen to know where the Sinn Féin election posters had been printed, but they bore no excited questions about the future. But I didn't need to hear any election promises from these young men: to a boy like me, used to nothing but the dullness of this stuffy town, the very sight of them was a promise of bigger, brighter things in other places. The young men hung around together in groups, smoking ready-rolled cigarettes, and they seemed to spend a lot of their time in Irishtown. There was a challenge in the way they walked, the way they dressed, even in the way they stood. To our provincial eyes they were glamour itself, but once my eyes had grown used to the glamour I noticed another thing about the way these men walked and stood and held themselves: I noticed that they were tough-looking men under their city ways, and though they often smiled, their eyes – especially when they saw a policeman – could get narrow and cold. And the police, though they kept a wary eye on the strange young men, never interfered with them on the streets, even on the streets of Irishtown. It struck me that these strangers were quite ready to have a go at the police if they were interfered with. That was such an odd idea for me that it took me some time to believe it; but the police obviously felt it too. These young strangers walked cockily around the town with the air of ownership, and no policeman interfered with them. That impressed me very much. So there was, after all, something besides respectability itself that the Royal Irish Constabulary respected. Or so I thought. But it wasn't respect, it was something else: wariness. And under the wariness, when the gloves came off, it was fear.

This was shown to me on the day before the big election meeting. I was playing cowboys with a few of the lads on the fairgreen at the far end of town that day – the far end, that is to say, from any place I was likely to be seen by my mother. I was playing, as ever, with my Irishtown friends. We had old bits of sticks for guns. I had broken my own stick into two short, curved pieces, and stuck them as pistols in my belt. I was Two-gun Tex Doherty, king of the wild prairies, except that I'd just been ambushed and shot down by Mickey Farrell as a whooping Indian brave.

I was dying nobly in the grass, taking my time about it, when I noticed Tom Farrell and two of the young strangers rounding a corner from the direction of Irishtown. They made an odd little procession. One of the strangers was carrying what looked like a bundle of newspapers, another a big galvanised bucket with the handle of a whitewash brush sticking out of it. Tom Farrell himself – Tom who'd been almost alone among the young men of Irishtown in having no interest in Gaelic games – was carrying a hurley.

It was one of the strangers who took my attention, though – the man who carried the bundle of papers. I'd already singled him out from seeing him around the town. He was a short little man. His cockiness made him stand out even among the company he kept. Alone among them, I'd never seen him give a policeman a dirty look – he only smiled at them, a bland, secret smile that was more insulting than any glower. All the other newcomers seemed to defer to him, and I'd taken it that he was some kind of leader among them.

Mickey Farrell stopped short when he saw the men coming.

'Begob,' he said, 'they must be very sure of themselves.'

'What are they at?' I asked him.

'They're putting up posters about the meeting,' Mickey said. 'That's what it looks like, anyhow.'

That explained the bundle of papers and the bucket. So here at last were at least some of the mysterious bill-stickers, whom Phil Murphy's men had never been able to find – 'the Scarlet Pimpernels of Irishtown,' as my father called them.

There was a block of old, half-derelict houses on the corner of the Green near where we boys were standing, their roofs broken and their doors and windows boarded up. The four young men made their way over towards these. Tom Farrell called out to us cheerfully.

'There's the hard men,' he said. 'Is it war, or is it a game of cowboys?'

I remembered that question many times later, after the shooting war started. It was a question that a lot of very serious people in Ireland were asking themselves then, though I didn't know it. When Tom asked it, of course, it was only a joking remark. We all laughed and ran over to Tom. It was a chance to have a closer look at his exotic friends.

I couldn't take Tom Farrell seriously as a political

candidate. Politicians were old, and solid, and respectable (in my mother's terms), and talked rubbish they obviously didn't believe in. Tom was young, hardly more than a boy himself, and if he talked nonsense itself, he was passionate about it. He had a way of throwing back his head and laughing at the smallest funny thing. He seemed too lively for politics. It seemed like a game he was playing, the way we played cowboys.

'It's cowboys, Tom,' I said to him. 'And your brother is after shooting me.'

Tom Farrell reached over and pulled one of my 'guns' from my belt. He held the stick up and pretended to sight down the barrel of a gun.

'Bang!' he said. Then he reversed it and let on to examine it critically. 'I do believe there's dirt in your barrel,' he said to me. 'It's a good thing you were never in the Citizens' Army. Poor ould Seán Connolly would have had your guts for garters if he saw you with a weapon in that state.'

He turned to the short stranger and gestured at me with the stick.

'This is Pat Doherty, Jamesy,' he said. 'His Da is Tim Doherty, the printer.'

The man called Jamesy grinned at me. 'How are you, Pat boy?' he said. 'Give us a look at your pistol.'

He reached out and took the old bit of a stick from Tom Farrell's hand, and he too pretended to examine it. He clicked his tongue.

'Shocking,' he said. 'Absolutely shocking.'

His speech had a singing quality to it, an accent alien to the local one. I knew it was a southern sound, but didn't know enough to place it any better than that.

'Put the chap on a charge, Jamesy,' said the third young man, a rail-thin lamppost of a fellow with his cap pulled down over one eye. I grinned, happy to be accepted by these strangers from another world, thrilling fearfully at the thought of what my mother would say if she saw me, almost wishing that she could.

Suddenly Mickey Farrell pushed past me and grabbed his brother's sleeve, hissing a warning.

'Peelers, Tom!' he said.

Everyone looked around. It was only one policeman, but not just any of them: it was Phil Murphy himself, advancing on us from the other end of the fairgreen, grim in his massive authority and staring straight at us where we stood. You could see him straighten even more as he came, making a bee-line for the group of us there – not that he noticed us boys, of course: his eyes were fastened on the three young men, and on the posters and paste-bucket they carried so openly.

No-one said anything. I was terrified. For all their cockiness, I imagined the young men were in for the mother and father of all hidings at the very least. Giving sneering looks to ordinary policemen was one thing, but Phil Murphy was no ordinary policeman; sneering looks, to Phil Murphy, would be like a red rag to a bull. The whole business with the posters, and his failure to find the bill-stickers, had made him, for the first time ever, a bit of a laughing-stock in the town. And no-one made a laughing-stock out of Phil Murphy, least of all an Irishtowner like Tom Farrell.

I half-expected the three young men to run, but there was no sign from them that they realised their danger. Even Tom, who had good cause to know the sergeant's ways, seemed alarmingly unworried. Mickey Farrell grabbed his brother's sleeve and shook it.

'Go!' Mickey hissed. 'You can still get around the corner. He'll never catch youse in the lanes.'

Tom gave him the strangest look that, to this day, I've ever seen pass between one brother and another. It was a calm, half-smiling look, and though his eyes were on Mickey's face there was absolutely no sign of recognition in them. I've often thought about that look since, and tried to put a name to it. I still couldn't do that for certain, but I have my suspicions. I think it was the look of someone who'd been waiting for something for a long time, and who thought that the thing they were waiting for had finally arrived. Mickey told me one time, a few years later, that when he saw that look he realised he didn't really know his brother at all.

'Don't worry, little fella,' Tom said gently to his brother. 'I'm sober this time.'

The third man had been looking calmly at the advancing King.

'Begod,' he said, 'but isn't he the fine figure of a man all the same?'

'He've a fine figure of a belly anyhow,' the man called Jamesy said breezily. 'Look at the bulge of it under that tunic.'

'Bacon and cabbage,' Tom Farrell murmured dreamily, and there was a strange, almost fond tone in his voice that, for no reason I knew, really frightened me. 'Bacon and cabbage, and pints of good black porter got for free off of grateful publicans.'

And lardy cake, he might have added, given by respectable women of the town.

We boys, without thinking or talking about it, had drawn back a little bit from the three Sinn Féiners. It wasn't that we were deserting them – God forbid! But for all that he made no threatening movements, there was something so nakedly dangerous in Phil Murphy's purposeful advance that, with every step he took, a sort of fog of violence seemed to thicken in the air. That may sound daft, I don't know. It didn't seem daft then. Maybe you've heard people talk of an atmosphere that you could cut with a knife; well, there of the fairgreen that day, as Phil Murphy came up to the three young Sinn Féiners, there was an atmosphere you could have cut with a soupspoon. The sergeant never took his eyes off the group of young men the whole time he came on, and the eyes were fixed on Tom Farrell in particular. The three men, in their turn, just stood easily there, and watched him coming. When he reached them, Murphy stopped. He towered over Tom, who was the tallest of the three.

'So it's you that's been defacing public property, Farrell,' he said. 'I suspected as much. Well, I caught you red-handed now.' He looked contemptuously at the other two men. 'Who's your go-boy pals?' he asked.

Tom said nothing at all, only smiled up at him with the same dreamy smile he'd given Mickey. There was silence for a time, and in the silence Phil Murphy's red face grew redder and darker. His hanging hands balled themselves into fists, and he seemed about to clout Tom Farrell there and then.

'Well?' he barked after a while. 'Are you deaf as well as stupid? I asked you a question – who's your friends?'

The small man called Jamesy slid between Tom and Murphy.

'You'll have to forgive poor Tom, sergeant,' he said to Murphy. His voice was soft and almost ingratiating. 'Truth to tell, you hit the nail on the head: Tom's hearing *is* a bit damaged – ever since he was attacked up a lane by some cowardly ruffians one night a few months ago. He's a game lad, but it was three against one, and they laid into him something terrible. Sure, the poor lad is hardly the better of it yet. He still has a ringing in his ears.' He sighed. 'There are some real desperadoes in these parts, sergeant,' he said. 'I blame the times that are in it. I don't envy you the job of keeping the peace.'

Phil Murphy stared at the small, slight man in front of

him. Jamesy had spoken perfectly civilly, but somehow you could hear in his innocent words the most insolent of sneers. Certainly Phil Murphy had heard it.

'Desperadoes?' Murphy said. 'We have no desperadoes here. Only a few jumped-up corner boys with big ideas of themselves. But we do try to teach them the error of their ways, so we do. And I still haven't been told who you two are.'

'You first,' Jamesy said.

Murphy stared at him. 'What?' he said. He sounded shocked.

'You tell us your name first. It's only politeness.'

Murphy's face was growing dark. This little stranger clearly wasn't afraid of him. If anything, he seemed to find the big policeman amusing. That was not a thing that Phil Murphy liked. He'd lost face over the election posters matter; now here was one of the culprits, jeering him.

'I'm the police sergeant!' Murphy spat. 'Isn't that enough for you? Or don't you have police sergeants in whatever Cork sewer you crawled out of?'

The little smile never left Jamesy's face. For all that their every exchange sounded laced with menace, he acted as though he and the sergeant were two friends bantering with each other on a street corner.

'Oh we do,' he said now. 'We do have police sergeants in the Cork sewer I crawled out of. Only, do you see, they know their place.'

Murphy flinched as though Jamesy had struck him. Beside me I heard Mickey Farrell draw in a startled breath. I doubted that anyone had ever spoken like that to Phil Murphy before, at least not since he put on a police uniform.

'What?' Phil Murphy said again. It was as though he hoped he'd misheard the little stranger.

'They – know – their – place,' Jamesy repeated, slowly and carefully. 'They're not so – *impertinent.*'

The insult was there now, naked and unmistakable. Phil Murphy's eyes flared with an ugly light. His face went a dark, dark red. I saw his hand reach up towards the long truncheon that he always wore on his belt.

'By God!' he said, almost to himself. 'By God!'

Jamesy kept smiling that same, friendly smile. He smiled it as he saw Murphy's hand reach for the truncheon, and he smiled it as his own hand snaked up and, in a single slick movement, pulled a long-barrelled black revolver from inside his coat. We boys – all of us, independently – gasped. That was a real gun, there on our fairgreen: a real pistol, presumably with bullets in it. Jamesy put the muzzle of the revolver squarely against the bottle-green cloth of the tunic covering Phil Murphy's chest. He had to reach up to do it. The sergeant's big hand froze an inch from the handle of his truncheon. His eyes bulged, and he stared down at the pistol with a look of absolute astonishment on his face. His mouth opened under his ragged red moustache, but no sound came out of it.

'Touch that truncheon,' Jamesy said in the same mild, friendly voice, 'and I'll blow a hole in you that a pigeon could fly through – if it didn't mind getting its wings wet.'

Phil Murphy's bulging eyes rose from the pistol to the still-smiling face of the man who held it. They went back down to the pistol, and then back up to the face. He simply didn't seem to believe what he was seeing. His mouth worked, but still nothing came out. His face wasn't dark red any more, nor even pale red: it was white.

'Now,' Jamesy said with mild satisfaction. '*Now* you look more like a police sergeant.'

Tom Farrell moved to stand in front of Phil Murphy, who looked at him blankly. The sergeant was like a man who'd been in an accident and was still dazed. He was in shock. Tom Farrell smiled at him. He reached up with one hand and took Murphy's helmet off his head. He had to stand on tiptoe to do it. He hefted the helmet in one hand, and in the other he hefted the hurley he held. He considered them both. Then he threw the sergeant's helmet in the air and hit it a savage belt of the hurley. The helmet flew up through the air and bounced off the roadway a good twenty yards away. Murphy stared after it, blinking. Then he turned empty eyes to look at Tom Farrell.

'That was my helmet,' he said. There was a catch in his voice, almost like a little child that was going to cry.

'Count yourself lucky,' Jamesy said coolly, 'that it wasn't your head.'

Murphy looked at him with that same blank look on his face. He seemed to have completely forgotten the gun stuck in his chest. Jamesy ground it into his tunic, to remind him it was there.

'On your knees,' he said.

Phil Murphy stared at him. He didn't seem to understand.

'Get down on your knees!' Jamesy said. 'NOW!'

His voice was suddenly cold.

Phil Murphy looked like he was going to say something, but he changed his mind. Slowly, stiffly, almost humbly, he sank to his knees on the roadway.

'Sure, you wouldn't shoot me, boys,' he said. 'I never done anything to deserve that.'

I was shocked by the humility in his voice. He looked up at the young men with a terrible, lost look in his eyes, like a man whose whole world had been taken away from him. Even if I did hate Phil Murphy, I hated it even more to see him like that. I hated the look on his face.

'Will we shoot him, do you think, Tom?' Jamesy asked Tom Farrell. His tone was conversational again.

Tom Farrell stood looking down at Phil Murphy's bare head, bent now, so that you could see a big spot of bald, naked skin gleaming white through the red hair. Tom hefted the hurley again, and for a terrible second I thought he was going to pull on Phil Murphy's head with it, in the same savage way that he'd pulled on the helmet. There was a look of downright gloating on Tom Farrell's face, a look I hated seeing as much as I hated seeing Murphy humbled, and with – it seemed to me then – as little reason. But something mean and cruel stood out plain on Tom's face at that moment – the hatred, I suppose, bred in Irishtown blood by generations of being thought of as hardly more than vermin. But then Tom seemed to take possession of himself; the look faded, and his face became again the one I knew.

'Look up at me, Phil Murphy,' Tom said.

Phil Murphy looked up, and I was disgusted and horrified to see that he was crying. There were tears running down his big face. His whole world had been turned upside down in the space of a couple of seconds. He thought he was going to die there in the dust of the street, and he didn't want to. Beside me I heard Mickey Farrell and several of the other Irishtown boys snigger, but I saw nothing to snigger about. I didn't like seeing men in this situation. It made all of them *cheap*, somehow, and I didn't think any of them – even Phil Murphy – deserved it. But then, I suppose, I had the leisure to feel like that: I wasn't from Irishtown, and the terror of Murphy I felt was of a different kind from the terror the Irishtowners knew. All other things being equal, it was unlikely, in the ordinary run of things, that he and his cronies would ever beat me up in a dark alley: I was far too respectable for that to be an option, at least in the world we had known before now. Though it was obvious from the scene in front of me, even to my young eyes, that that world had suddenly changed.

'What's it to be, Tom?' Jamesy said. His revolver was pointing at Phil Murphy's head. He placed the muzzle of the gun now between Murphy's bushy red eyebrows, and he pulled back the hammer. I jumped at the sound of the dry metal click. A shot itself couldn't have been any louder. There seemed to be no other sound in the world.

Phil Murphy started blubbering. There's no other word for it. His face crumpled up, and under his ragged moustache his lips made strange, ugly shapes. He was sure, I knew, that he was going to die. I was sure of it myself.

'For God's sake, don't kill me!' Phil Murphy said. He was begging. There was a whiney sound in his voice that I would never have imagined it could have. The three young men looked at him with no feeling in their eyes except, maybe, a sort of curiosity. They had the look almost of little kids playing with a new toy, trying it out to see what they could make it do.

'I've a poor widowed mother,' Phil Murphy pleaded, 'and I'm her only support.'

Jamesy raised his eyebrows.

'She'd do better,' he said, 'to look for a steadier prospect, so. I don't think your job is a secure one, sergeant.' He looked at Tom Farrell. 'Well?' he asked.

Tom Farrell leaned down until his face was right up

against Phil Murphy's. Murphy's face, raddled with tears and with fear, looked suddenly old, fat and weak.

'You're looking at the next Member of Parliament for this constituency,' Tom Farrell said. Then, like a teacher: 'What are you looking at?'

'The next ...' Phil Murphy's tongue stumbled over the words. He had trouble getting them out. 'The next Member ... of P-Parliament for ... this constituency.'

Tom Farrell nodded. 'You'll leave me alone,' he said. 'What will you do?'

'I'll leave you alone.'

'You'll leave my friends alone too.'

'I'll ... I'll leave your friends alone.'

'You and your men will stay away from the election meeting tomorrow. And you'll stay out of Irishtown. If you show your face there even once before election day, we'll blow it off of you. And the same goes for any other peeler in this town. Do you hear me, Phil Murphy?'

'I do, Tom, I do.'

Phil Murphy had suddenly realised that he wasn't going to die. His voice bubbled with gratitude. He reached out his two big hands and grabbed one of Tom Farrell's. He bent his wet face and, in an act that disgusted me to my stomach, he kissed it.

'God bless you, Tom!' Phil Murphy said. 'God Bless you! May his own blessed Mother look down on you. And thank you, son. Thank you!'

Beside me my Irishtown friends were still sniggering, but they mightn't have existed at all for all the notice that Phil Murphy took of them. Jamesy uncocked and put up his revolver, but didn't yet put it back inside his coat.

'Get up, now,' he said almost gently to Phil Murphy. 'Get up, and turn around, and go away. Stay clear of us, and tell your men to do the same. If you do that, then maybe – just maybe – we won't kill you. Do anything else and you're a dead man. Do you understand?'

Phil Murphy got to his feet, grovelling. In the space of a couple of minutes he seemed to have aged by twenty years. When he stood up he still towered over all three of them, but even so he seemed smaller than any of them. Even a little gun, I suppose, is bigger than any man; and Jamesy's gun wasn't little.

'I do, sir,' Phil Murphy said. 'I understand you, and I'll do everything just as you say.'

I had never heard him sound so keen to please.

'That's my boy,' Jamesy said. His breezy manner had hardly changed during the entire interlude.

Phil Murphy looked as though he were about to say something else, but he didn't. He just turned around and walked back the way he had come. At first he walked with slumped shoulders, but as he went he straightened up, and his step brightened, and by the time he disappeared around the corner he was striding purposefully along. He strode, though, without his helmet, which still lay in the roadway where it had fallen. It was a thing unknown for a police sergeant to be seen in public without his helmet; it was sure to be noticed.

The rest of us, men and boys alike, stood staring after Phil Murphy till he disappeared. No-one said anything. Then Jamesy hefted the revolver in his hand and looked at Tom Farrell.

'What did I tell you?' he asked. 'A gun makes all the difference.'

But Tom Farrell had come back to the real world.

'Except,' he said, 'that he's gone back to the barracks now, and there's guns there too. How do we know he won't come back with his men and their carbines?'

Jamesy smiled.

'He won't,' he said.

'But what if he does?'

'Then we'll shoot him. And anyone with him. And then we'll have more guns, and that will make even more of a difference.'

'And if they come to the meeting tomorrow?'

'If they come to the meeting tomorrow then we'll be ready for them. Right now we have posters to put up.'

The third man had gone off and fetched Phil Murphy's helmet. He brought it back and held it out to Tom.

'A souvenir for you,' he said.

Tom spat. 'I don't want it,' he said. He was almost snarling.

The man held the helmet out towards us boys.

'How about you lads? Do you fancy a game of policemen?'

The Irishtown boys mobbed him, clamouring for the helmet. I hung back, not wanting to touch it, but not knowing why. I felt completely confused, and when I looked at the eagerness of my friends I felt more alone than I'd ever done in my whole life. The three young men went about their business, leaving us boys on the green. The others soon invented a new game, where one boy got to wear the helmet and be the policemen, while the other boys chased him and, when they caught him, beat him up. I didn't join in: it seemed too much like a reverse version of the game that Phil Murphy and his constables had played with Tom Farrell the night he came back. My feelings were all mixed up, and I didn't understand them. When Mickey Farrell noticed my odd mood, and asked if I was all right, I said I had a pain in my stomach, and was going home to lie down. I went off for a long walk on my own.

I walked the town for hours before I went home. There I was so quiet and distracted that my mother thought I was sick. She felt my forehead and declared me feverish. She sent me to bed, where I lay for a long time, thinking. Later, my father came in to see me. He could see that, whatever was wrong with me, it wasn't a physical thing. When he asked me whether anything had happened to upset me, I told him the whole story. He sat on my bed and he listened in silence, only prompting me very gently when I faltered. By the time I finished, he had his elbows on his knees and his head between his hands.

'My God,' he said after a while. 'Has it finally come to this?'

'To what, Daddy?' I asked him. I'd turned the events of the afternoon over and over in my mind, trying to understand what had disgusted me about them so. Phil Murphy, whom I hated, had got his come-uppance. I felt that I should have been glad. But I wasn't glad at all. Instead I felt ashamed, as though I'd seen some awful thing I shouldn't see. But all I'd seen was the blubbering face of the ex-King of Irishtown, humbled by a young man with a gun. I had no reason to feel any sympathy for Phil Murphy – indeed, I didn't feel any. I didn't even pity him. But I felt no triumph either, nor even pleasure at his downfall. What I felt instead was that shame, and a kind of disgust. That was what I couldn't understand.

'What did I see today, Daddy?' I asked my father. It was a question I'd never have asked my mother. I wouldn't have dreamed even of saying a word to her about the events on the fairgreen. I knew, in any case, exactly how she would have interpreted them. My father, though, was different. He sat and thought about my question for a good while without saying anything. Then he reached over and put his arm around my shoulder and – eleven years old though I was, and disliking soft stuff – I burrowed gratefully into his warm, strong embrace that smelled vaguely of ink and tobacco.

'I think, son,' he said, 'that you saw something very few people ever get to see.'

That, of course, was perfectly true: I'd seen a pistol produced in our town, and I'd seen Phil Murphy frightened and crying. I'd hoped for something a bit more, though, from my father. I'd hoped for something that would help me understand my feelings. But when, disappointedly, I admitted as much, he hugged me even tighter.

'That's not what I meant at all, son,' he said. 'Not at all. I wish it was.'

'What, then?' I asked him. I desperately wanted to know. 'What did you mean? What did I see?'

'The future,' my father said, and his voice was every bit as sad and lonesome as I'd felt all afternoon. 'I think you saw the future.'

I knew what he meant and I didn't know what he meant, all at the same time. There was nothing to say. So the two of us sat on my bed, huddled and silent, and listened through the closed door to the muffled sound of my mother's voice off in the house somewhere, giving out to the maid.

Dead Man's Music

I was thirteen years old when I found the dead man in the barn, but I remember it like it was yesterday. I'd seen dead people before, of course – my grandfather, the time we got him dead in the chair, and young Murt Breen that time the horse kicked him in the head. Murt had lain in the churned-up muck of Carty's yard and there wasn't a mark to be seen on him, but his eyes sort of fluttered and he called out real loud for his mammy one time and then he died. When the men picked him up he was all floppy, and nearly slithered out of their arms. He was sixteen then, and he'd been a great hurler. His team did very bad the year after, missing his skill.

I'd seen a dead woman one time too, when I was ten. It was Mary Callaghan's daughter Rose, that went missing on the hill. I was the one found her caught in the weeds at a bend in Murray's stream. Her long hair was flowing in the water and the little fishes were darting in and out of it. The searchers found me standing there looking at her, and they thought I was too frightened to shout out. But really I'd been thinking how peaceful she looked, swaying there in the stream like she was dancing to a music the rest of us couldn't hear – fairy music, dead men's music – some tune, anyhow, that left her at peace. She'd been funny in her head, Rose Callaghan, and I'd never seen her looking peaceful before. There was a kind of beauty off her face there in the water, if that doesn't sound soft. Her eyes were wide open, and they had a look in them like she was seeing something lovely and far-off, like she was after being let look at some special secret we poor live ones couldn't see.

I said nothing about that to anyone, though. They'd have thought I was mad. We children used to catch them little fishes in that stream – 'minnies', we called them. Our fathers and mothers had done the same thing, and their fathers and mothers back as far as ould god's time. But I never felt right doing it after that. I'd look at the ones that I'd caught and wonder whether any of them had swum in Rose Callaghan's hair. It took the good out of catching them.

What I'd never seen – till I found the man in the barn – was a person so obviously killed on purpose by other people. The man that I found in the barn didn't look peaceful at all. I'd never seen a dead person so bloody. And that will show you that I'd led a quiet life, because men were killing each other by the new time in Ireland then.

It was the blood I saw first – a big slawm of it there in the dust, like someone was after dragging a slaughtered pig across the floor of the barn. But I knew there'd been no pigs slaughtered there. I followed the trail with my eyes and at the end of it I saw a man with a scarlet face, wearing a scarlet shirt, lying in the straw in the corner. I can picture it this minute. I knew straight away that his face and his shirt weren't scarlet by nature, only dyed that way with the blood. It's funny, I suppose, that I still call him the dead man, because of course as it turned out he wasn't dead at all. But that's the way I thought of him when I saw him first, because I couldn't imagine that something so bloody could be alive. But he wasn't dead – not in the way that Murt Breen and Rose Callaghan were dead anyhow. And now, at my age, I'd hardly even call him a man – he can't have been more than twenty, though that was hard to see then under the mask of dirt and blood.

Later, after he was cleaned up and when he was hiding in our hayloft till he was strong enough to travel, I still thought of him as the dead man. It was something dead in his eyes, something cold and far away. Eyes were made to look out, to look out and to look forward. But even when he was all cleaned up and getting better, the dead man's eyes – even when they were looking straight at you – seemed to be looking inwards, and to be looking back. And what they were looking at wasn't what Rose Callaghan had been looking at: it was nothing beautiful, and it wasn't far away. Sometimes too when you'd talk to him he wouldn't even hear you. It was like he was listening to something else, something inside of him. Maybe it was another kind of dead man's music he was hearing. If so, then I'm glad I never heard it, because it surely wasn't peaceful like Rose Callaghan's.

The time that I found him, anyhow, I didn't know he wasn't dead in the ordinary way. He was dressed in civilian clothes, and I suppose I just assumed the Tans or soldiers had shot him. There was no sign around his neck saying 'SPIES AND TRAITORS BEWARE', so it didn't look like a rebel job. The rebels, in any case, left the bodies of people they killed in more public places. Not that I was any great expert – there'd been no killings yet around our way that time. But I'd listened to my father when he read the newspapers out at night around the fire. I liked to know what was going on, and what was going on in Ireland then was murder and madness. The adults would shake their heads at news of fresh burnings and ambushes and robberies and executions, but we children found it exciting. There was no television then, of course, nor even radio. There wasn't even a picture house or anything around that we could go to. And farm life could get awful tedious sometimes, so a bit of excitement was always welcome.

I stood looking at the dead man for a minute, that morning I found him, then I thought I should go and tell someone. I didn't want anyone to blame me for anything. My father was in the house getting ready to go into town on some bit of business. On my way to the house I noticed bloodstains in the yard. I hadn't seen them on the way in.

They weren't big, which meant that the dead man had still been walking or at least staggering when he'd come through there.

When I ran into the kitchen my little brothers, Tim and Matt, were dancing around my father's feet begging him to bring sweets back from the town. Daddy was teasing them, asking them why he should bother. His old black hat was on the back of his head, and his pipe in his hand.

'What sort of childer am I rearing,' Daddy said, 'that would sell their souls for a bit of Peggy's Leg?'

Peggy's Leg was a sort of a sweet you could get nearly anywhere then. I don't think you can get it at all now.

'Daddy!' I said. 'Daddy! There's a man!'

The three of them looked at me, standing in the middle of the floor, dancing with the thrill of my news.

'What man?' my father said.

'A dead man,' I said. 'A dead man covered with blood in the barn.'

I'd hardly got the words out before Tim and Matt, squealing with excitement, ran out past me to get a look. It wasn't every day that started off with such a marvel. My father looked from me to them and back. Then he roared after them to stop, but they were already gone.

'A dead man,' he said flatly to me.

'Dead,' I said. 'And all bloody. The floor looks like a dead pig is after being dragged across it.'

My father said a curse-word and stalked out to look. I

went after him. When we got to the barn Tim and Matt were standing with their arms around each other, staring at the man in the straw. My father said the same word again.

'This is exactly what I need,' he said then, but you could tell he meant the very opposite.

'Sure he've nothing to do with us, Daddy,' I said. 'It's not our fault he died here. We didn't kill him.'

My father scowled at me.

'Look at his chest,' he said.

I looked, but all I saw was torn, bloody cloth.

'You eejit,' my father said. 'Can't you see that he's breathing?'

When I looked again carefully I saw the little rise and fall of the bloody chest. But still I didn't see why that was bad: a live man, surely, was better than a dead one.

'We'll go for the police,' I said. 'They'll sort it out.'

I'd never thought the fighting in the country had anything to do with us. We weren't political. We raised our animals and watched the weather in dread of a lost crop. What did it matter to us who ran things in Dublin? What had Dublin to do with us? You kept your head down and got on with your work – there was always plenty of that to keep you busy, and never enough time to do it all. That was the way that we lived around these parts then.

But my father looked at me now like I'd sprouted a second head.

'What am I rearing?' he said. 'Are you mad as well as

stupid? There was never an informer in our family!' He looked angrily at the bloody man. 'It's an unhealthy life anyhow, informing,' he muttered. 'Unhealthy and short.'

'What informing?' I said. 'We found a man. We should tell the police. That's not informing, is it?'

'Talking to the peelers when you don't have to,' my father said, 'is enough to get you called an informer.'

'But look at the blood,' I said. 'If he's not dead itself then he can't be far off it. If we get the police after he dies then we can't be blamed, can we?'

'Shut up,' my father said. 'I'm thinking.'

He took his chin between the thumb and forefinger of one hand and rubbed it. It was a way he had, as though he was trying to rub an answer out of the blue-shadowed flesh.

'This man is hurted,' he said finally. 'We can't just let him die. But he's even more trouble alive, that's for sure.'

Tim and Matt were standing in front of him, looking at the man, squirming with excitement. Their heads leaned close together, whispering. Da gave both of them a mild clatter on the backs of their heads.

'Youse get out of here,' he said. 'Tell your Ma to heat some water.'

He turned to me. 'I've the horse in the yard,' he said, 'ready to put in the trap. You ride down to Murrays' and tell Paddy what's after happening. Do whatever he tells you. Say nothing to anyone else you meet, mind, apart from the Murrays – do you hear me?'

I nearly fainted with pleasure. An adventure!

'I won't tell a sinner, Da,' I said. 'I swear to God. Will Paddy Murray know what to do?'

Da looked hard at the dying man and sighed.

'He'd bloody better,' he said. 'Because I don't.'

* * *

I was a bit surprised at the man I was sent to fetch. I wouldn't have expected Paddy Murray to know much about anything beyond dogs, horses and dances. The Murrays were our nearest neighbours. Their farmhouse was about a mile down the lane. They were a big, prosperous family of six sons. One of the sons was a priest in America, the rest lived at home and worked the farm. Paddy was the youngest, and he was known locally as a bit of a playboy. He was a handsome man of about thirty, very popular but not regarded as the steadiest of men. He seemed to live for his own enjoyment, and took nothing seriously. He had a joke for every occasion. He was the last man I'd have thought of turning to at a time like this.

I rode our horse Jessie down the lanes to Murrays'. It was still early, and I met no-one on the way. Across the valley I could see a cart slowly descending the lane on the far slope, and I could see the smoke rising from the chimneys of the scattered homesteads on the side of the far mountain. It was a cold, sunny day in November, and the air was full of a brittle winter light. Jessie's big hooves plopped in the muck of the lane, and the bare hedges still dripped from the last night's rain. I noticed all of these things very clearly on that short ride, and I noticed them as though I was seeing them for the first time. And yet I'd seen them all a thousand times before, because this was all the world I knew.

I thought about the dead man in the stable, the dead man who wasn't quite dead. I finally saw what was troubling my father. Dead or alive, the man was trouble. In fact, as my father had realised, he was more trouble alive than dead. If the worst came to the worst, you could dump a dead body. But the dead man hadn't even had the manners to die properly. I know that might sound cruel, but they were cruel times. All times are cruel to people who only scratch a living at the best of times. We had enough to do looking after our own. We didn't know the dead man, and he was none of our business, but now he was very much our problem. If he'd been involved in some outrage then the British would punish the whole area for harbouring him. It wasn't fair, but it was their way. There would be no use in explaining things. Tans didn't listen to explanations, it wasn't their job. Their job, so far as I knew, was to frighten people. It had never made sense to me, but it seemed to make sense to them. They were good at it, too. When I looked at the scattered houses on the slopes across the valley, I tried to picture them burning. That was what the Tans would do, and my own home would be the first to go.

At least the dead man wasn't a problem for our family

alone. The valley people were careful and silent and sensible, and they kept their own counsel; but when there was a shared threat they would stick together. I couldn't feel that this fighting had anything to do with any of us, to whom only the weather and the farm prices mattered; but if having the dead man on our hands made him our business, then at least our own business was a thing we could look after. The valley people had a saying about a man: *He sees what he sees and he says what he says,* they'd say, *but he never says the half of what he sees.* When they said that of a man, it was said with approval.

When I turned into Murrays' yard Paddy and his brother Har were there looking at the engine of Paddy's Ford motor car. It was his own car, for his own use, and not a farm machine. Paddy rented the car out sometimes, as a hackney, but that had been only an excuse for buying it. Mainly he used it to ferry himself and his friends around. People looked on it as an extravagance.

'How do his Ma and Da let him waste money like that?' the old people used to say. 'Is it any wonder he's gone to the bad, and he so spoiled.'

Paddy and Har had heard the horse coming, and were looking up when we came through the gate. I told them what had happened. Har Murray was about forty, and I expected him to take charge of any response, but he said nothing. Paddy, on the other hand, kept interrupting me with short, serious questions. Har deferred to him, watching his brother's reactions.

'Right,' said Paddy when I'd done. 'Har, get the bits and pieces from the house. We'll drive up.'

Har went inside. Paddy Murray folded down the bonnet of his car. He looked as serious as he'd sounded. It wasn't the Paddy Murray I was used to. There was no joking now.

'You ride down to Hogans',' he said to me. 'Find Jamesy or Beeda and tell them what's after happening. If they're not there, tell Marian. You can trust her.'

It was another mile or so down the lane to Hogans'. They had a smaller farm of poorish land, the fields too scattered to be managed easily. Old Bridgie Hogan was a widow, and depended on her two sons to run the place. Her daughter Marian was always very nice to me. Bridgie's hands were crippled now with the arthritis, and Marian ran the house. She was in the kitchen with Beeda when I came in. Marian was the local beauty. Someone had even written a song about her. One day at a fair Jamesy Hogan had heard someone singing the song, and he'd knocked the singer down. Jamesy had a sup taken that day, it being a fairday, but he'd probably have tackled the singer anyway, though the man probably meant no harm. They were a very close and jealous family, the Hogans, though I'd always found them friendly enough myself.

I wasted no time in giving my message. Beeda Hogan chewed his stained moustache and looked at me with his eyes half closed. He was a big man who always seemed amazed by anything he heard. He spoke mostly in exclamations: 'Be the hokey,' he'd say, or 'Be the livin' jinnet.' That was where he got his name, 'Beeda'. But he said nothing at all as he listened to me now, only chewed the ragged ends of his moustache. He was good with animals, Beeda was. He had cures for their ailments. People would bring their sick animals to Beeda before they'd think of going to an animal doctor.

'The poor wounded chap,' Marian said when I'd done. 'I'll go up with youse, Beeda.'

'No need. Sure, Jamesy and me can do anything you could,' Beeda said. 'Is Jamesy still up in the long field?'

'He's beyant in the haggard, I think,' Marian said.

'Go and get him then,' Beeda said. 'Tell him to get the guns. I'll get the trap ready.'

'Yerra, what do you want to waste the time for?' Marian asked. 'Get up on the pony the two of youse.'

'She won't carry the two of us that far,' Beeda said.

'Youse ride Jessie,' I said. 'She'll take the two of youse. I'll take the pony.'

Jessie was a big, powerful horse, as Beeda knew. He thought, chewing. He was the sort of a man whose face showed it when he was thinking. Apart from exclamations he was a man of few words. Then he nodded.

'Aye,' he said.

Marian had gone to fetch Jamesy. When Beeda and I went outside, he was already coming across the yard.

Marian walked along behind him. Jamesy was carrying a bundle wrapped in oilcloth. When he unwrapped it I saw a shotgun and an old fowling rifle that looked like an antique.

'Wrap them up again, ye fool,' Beeda said. 'There's eyes everywhere.'

'So long as the mouths stays shut,' Jamesy said, 'I've no fear of the eyes.'

'Wrap them up, anyhow,' Beeda said.

Jamesy wrapped the guns back up. The brothers mounted Jessie and set out, Jamesy holding the bundle between himself and Beeda. I made to go and fetch their pony, but Marian caught my shoulder.

'Do the chap above look hurted bad?' she asked me.

'I thought he was dead when I found him,' I said. 'He's all blood everywhere.'

She stared off at nothing.

'Did you know him?' she asked me.

'I don't know,' I said. I hadn't thought of it before. 'I didn't recognise him, but his face is all swelled up and bloody. You wouldn't know Beeda if you saw him in that state.'

'I pities the poor chaps that are out,' Marian said. 'I even pities the soldiers when they gets shot. It's no fit life for a man, fighting.'

I'd never thought about that, either, but I'd never needed to. Owning your own land and working it was all the life I thought fit. It was the way I'd been raised. My father had never taught me that lesson, at least not in so many words; but his whole existence shouted it out to the world.

'I'd better go,' I said. 'They might need me for something above.' And I didn't want to miss anything, though I didn't want to say that to Marian.

'Aye,' Marian said. 'I was only thinking out loud, anyhow. You know where the pony is, don't you?'

I did. It wasn't as though they had many outbuildings anyway. On the way back home I felt eyes on me, though I passed no houses and saw no people. The lane led uphill, and anyone travelling on it was visible to half the valley. I was sure the unusual comings and goings had been taken note of by people in the scattered houses and cottages. We had no secrets in our community. Nothing odd happened there that was not seen, because so little ever happened that was odd.

* * *

At the last turn in the lane before our gate I met Har Murray. He was up in the ditch watching the lane, and I didn't even see him till I was fornenst him. Har had a well-earned name as a poacher, and I suppose that taught you skills for which there were other uses. I would have gone past him if he hadn't called my name.

'Did you see anything quare?' he asked me. He was carrying a rifle.

'Divil a thing,' I told him. I couldn't tear my eyes off the gun. It looked very like the short carbines the police carried. Certainly it wasn't the sort of thing you ever saw round our way.

When I got to the house I found Paddy Murray's Ford parked in the yard. Jamesy Hogan was standing beside it holding the old fowling piece. He nodded to me as he took the pony.

'I hope you're not after being hard on the poor pony,' he said. 'She's all we have.'

I left him examining the animal and ran into the stable. Beeda Hogan was kneeling by the red man, wiping his face with a wet cloth, making him that bit less red. Blood is awful oily sometimes, after it's thickened a bit. They'd already cut off the dead man's shirt and had cleaned and bandaged his body-wounds. It was the first time I saw how young he looked, and how skinny.

My father was there with Paddy Murray. They looked round as I came in.

'Is he shot bad?' I asked them.

'He's not shot at all,' Paddy said. 'He was cut up with a bayonet or a knife.'

'Is he a rebel, then?' Bayonets sounded like soldiers' or Tans' work. It was said they tortured prisoners with them. Some of the Tans that I'd seen in the town on market days were a terrible rough-looking lot. You'd believe any cruelty of them.

'He's not from around here, anyhow,' my father said. 'Though I knows the cast of his face from someplace. He have soft hands, and city clothes.'

'I know who he is,' Paddy Murray said. 'He's one of our lads on a job from Dublin. He's from around these parts originally.'

'A townie, so,' my father said, sounding unimpressed. Townies were alien to us, livers of soft lives and doers of strange deeds. Their heads, my father always said, got filled with strange notions. It came, he thought, of having nothing to do. There was never any fear of that round our way. Round our way there was always plenty that had to be done.

'What's his name?' Daddy asked, but Paddy Murray shook his head.

'You're as well not knowing that, Myles,' he said.

I was amazed at the change in Paddy Murray. There was nothing of the playboy about him now. His whippet face was serious, and his eyes that always sparkled were cold and thinking.

'What I want to know,' my father said, 'is whether he can be moved. It looks like he loused up his job, whatever it was, and, if so, then the Tans will be atin' the country looking for him.'

Paddy Murray looked at the dead man.

'Maybe he loused up,' he said, 'and maybe he didn't. I suppose it depends on the state of the other fellas. But he's hurted bad. He's all cut up. Beeda can tend a few ould things in animals, but not something like this. This fella shouldn't be moved till after he sees a doctor.'

My father folded his arms and rubbed his chin.

'Lovely,' he said, not meaning it. 'Well, he didn't come far in that condition, that's for sure. Whatever he was doing, he was doing it near here. They'll be hunting for him soon.'

Paddy looked at him with no expression on his face. My father was a man who had no time for any politics. If a wounded rebel who'd done some devilment was found on his farm, the least we could expect was to have the place burned down around our ears. Beyond that, you never knew. Maybe my father would be arrested; maybe he'd be shot out of hand. It had happened.

'There was strangers moved into that ould cottage up the mountain,' my father said to Paddy. 'Up beyant on the estate land. English, they say.'

I'd heard talk of that myself. It had all happened very quietly, but nothing could be done secretly in an area like ours.

Paddy Murray said nothing to my father's words, only kept looking levelly at him. Then he went over and asked Beeda Hogan something in a low voice. Beeda made a face at him and shook his head. Paddy came back over.

'Beeda thinks he'll die if he's moved,' he said.

'Maybe he'll die anyhow,' my father said. 'He have my

sympathy if so, but I've no desire to go with him. I don't even know the man.'

He raised a big hand and pointed west, up the mountain.

'I follied his trail back a bit,' he said, 'He came across-country, and he left a trail that a blind fool could follow. Anyplace he stopped he left a lock of blood. I'm surprised he've any blood in him at all. If he came from that cottage, then that's a good three mile.'

I watched the two of them closely. Paddy Murray wanted the dead man to stay where he was, at least for now. My father – well, I was sure that he really did pity the man, the way he'd pity any wounded thing. But he had a farm and a family to think of.

Paddy Murray sucked his teeth in thought. I knew now that the Murrays and the Hogans were rebels. I hadn't known that before, and I was very surprised that I hadn't known it. I expected Paddy to threaten my father, and to back up that threat with guns. But I knew too that my father would take threats from nobody, armed or otherwise. Where the safety of farm and family were concerned, my father would have defied God himself. But Paddy Murray knew that too.

'God knows what's up beyant in that cottage,' he said. 'This chap must have done the job in some form or fashion, else you'd be up to your oxters in Black and Tans already. And if he done the job then we've time. The police left supplies at the cottage only yesterday, and they're only up there every two or three days.'

'Someone was hiding there, then,' my father said.

Paddy Murray shook his head. There was no need for my father to know any more.

'I'll organise the lads,' Paddy said. 'We'll clear up at the cottage and cover the trail.'

'There'll be bodies?' Daddy asked. I knew it wasn't really a question. The dead man had been doing some job that had led to him being carved up like a goose at Christmas: he obviously hadn't been up at the cottage delivering potatoes.

'If there's bodies,' Paddy said, 'we'll take them somewhere else. Make a trail down the far slope of the mountain, maybe, and leave them where they'll be found easy.'

My father nodded. They might have been discussing the price of cattle.

I knew the old cottage on the estate. I tried to imagine what might be up there, then stopped myself. The picture in my mind was full of blood.

'Don't leave them near houses,' My father said.

'I'm not a fool,' Paddy Murray said.

My father gave him a long, cool look. 'Maybe not,' he said. 'Maybe not.'

Paddy left that comment alone. My father looked around. He seemed surprised when he caught sight of me, as though he'd forgotten I was there.

'Mylie,' he said. He clapped a hand on my shoulder. 'You done well, son,' he said. 'Did you see anything odd on the road?'

I shook my head. I wanted to tell him about my feeling on the way back, about my sense of being watched. But that meant nothing. Of course I'd been watched: everything here was watched. It was just that this morning was the first time I'd thought about it. It was the first time I'd done something that might be better kept hidden, here on these bare hills where nothing could be hidden long. But here before me now were the Murrays and the Hogans suddenly revealed as rebels, when, no doubt, they'd been rebels all along. And I'd known nothing about that at all. I'd never even heard a whisper of it. This thing at least had been kept hidden on the hill, hidden from one boy at least.

Did the other people of the valley know about the Murrays and the Hogans? Of course they'd know. The Murrays and the Hogans ... and who knew how many more? I thought of the men of that valley, the young men who worked in their fields and played cards on winter nights in the kitchens of their scattered homesteads. I tried to guess which of them might also be involved in this work, to picture them out in the fields at night, at once hunted and hunting, bent on their dangerous games. I tried to imagine them killing people. They were all my neighbours, and yet I realised that day that I did not know them. And after that day, the feeling stayed. When I looked at a neighbour, a person I'd known all my life, I would wonder who they really were, and what they really knew. I suppose in a strange way you could say I grew up on that day.

*   *   *

As for the dead man in the stable, he recovered. He was moved very carefully to the hayloft, where a snug little cell was hollowed out for him in the hay. A reliable doctor was brought that night to examine him. He said the man had lost a lot of blood, but no vital organs had been damaged so far as he could tell. The man had been wounded by a knife, and not a bayonet, and that was good because a bayonet, with its long blade, would probably have done more damage. The doctor sewed the man up, and left a supply of morphia and antiseptic powders to be used on him. He came back a few times after.

The dead man was with us for a week and a half, and when he was well enough he ate food that we brought him. That came to be my job, and it was while I was bringing the food that I noticed the dead eyes he had. He didn't talk much, and then one morning he was gone.

On the afternoon of that first day, the day that I found the dead man, Paddy Murray led a group of ten men up through our haggard onto the hillside. My father told us to stay out of the way when they came, but from behind the net curtain of the bedroom window I watched them pass through, watching as I was sure I myself had been watched that morning. I knew every one of those men that passed by. I'd grown up knowing them. But there wasn't one of them I'd have guessed for a likely rebel if you'd asked me before. They were ordinary men, ordinary farmers. That day as they went up the hill they all carried guns. These men especially I could never look at in the same way afterwards; I felt as though I'd glimpsed through the net curtains some secret adult side of them, some side that a child should not see. And I felt that I'd never known a single one of them at all. Then my mother caught me peeking and gave me a puck in the head, and I ran upstairs and hid. But I was glad to go, because watching those men I'd seemed to feel a thing I could barely put into words: I'd seemed to feel my whole world slipping away.

We heard afterwards that two bodies were found in the river, clear across on the other side of the mountain. They were found in a car that had been driven right into the water, leaving a clear trail in the mucky ground from the old cottage on the estate land. The river was swollen by the winter rain, but it wasn't full enough to float the car downstream. Someone had seen it there and reported it, and a party of Tans and police had come and found it, with two dead men sitting in it, shot. There was a bit of a fuss, but then things quietened down.

In the year after that the British left, and we had a civil war. Of the men I'd seen go up our haggard that day, some took one side in that war and some took the other.

Four of them died, fighting on opposite sides, and two of those men were first cousins and had been brought up in each other's houses. Another of the four was Beeda Hogan. As for the dead man from the barn, I never saw him again, though I know he took the rebel side in the civil war and I know that he became well-known to the big world. I know that because a few years ago a fellow came here asking questions about him for a programme that he wanted to make for the television. Someone told him the dead man had been cared for in our barn one time, and the man came here to ask me about it because all the other people round here from that time are dead. I told the television man that I knew nothing. I'm a valley man, after all: I see what I see, and I say what I say, but I never say the half of what I see.

But it was true, too, in a way, what I told the television man: I really knew nothing about the dead man. For me his stay with us was just something that happened, like a kick from a horse or a storm when a storm was not expected. For me his stay with us meant nothing in itself; its importance lay in what it made me find out about my world. That world, of course, was small: it was made up only of the hillsides and the valley, and the people who lived there. Nobody makes television films about that world. But back then when the dead man came it was the only world I knew, or thought I knew; and the day that he came was the day I found out that I didn't know it at all.

And from that day to this, though I have lived a long life now, and spent much of it far away from this valley where I was born, I have never seen anything anywhere that surprised me more than that first great surprise, because I have never believed quite as completely in any world since.

Services Rendered

Mr Murphy, the neighbours agreed, looked the picture of health. They hadn't seen him look so well in years. If not for the fact that he was lying in a coffin with two pennies on his eyes, you might never even have guessed he was dead.

'I declare to God,' said Nellie Browne from next door, 'but it's nearly worth it. Wouldn't you welcome your death in the morning, all the same, if you thought you'd look half as well after?'

It wasn't all the doing of the undertakers' men, for all that they'd worked on Mr Murphy for an hour or more that morning with their paints and powders. Mr Murphy had died suddenly in his sleep, with no outward sign of illness at all – not so much as a sore throat or a cough. He'd gone to bed hale and hearty the night before, and this morning his wife had found him stone dead in the bed. His coffin lay on the table now in what the family described to visitors as 'the parlour'. Among themselves they just called it 'the room' because it was, apart from the back kitchen behind it, the only downstairs room in the house. Even the toilet was in the back yard.

The room wasn't a very big room, but, still, the coffin didn't take up all that much of it because it wasn't a very big coffin. And it wasn't a very big coffin because, for all that he'd been a loud man on occasion, Mr Murphy hadn't been a very big one. His mouth, his own brother Mick used to say, was the biggest thing about him – that and his heart. Certainly his mouth was the bit of himself that Mr Murphy had used most, whether giving out about the world and his family or filling it – when he could – with porter. It was the heart, though, that had worn out first – 'The ould ticker,' as Uncle Mick said, 'wasn't up to scratch.'

Mr Murphy's mouth had spent quite a bit of time lately talking about Mr Murphy's heart, mostly declaring it broken – or, as he himself put it, 'broke'.

'Me heart is broke,' he'd say, 'with the state of poor ould Ireland.'

No-one had taken him literally when he said it, of course. Mr Murphy's heart was always broke about something or other, whether it was the country, his income, or a bad hurling result for the local team. And his was by no means the only heart troubled by the state of the nation then, though of late the Murphys had more cause than many to be heartsore. Their two sons, Eddie and Myles, were in the Volunteers, and since martial law had been extended to the whole country they had, like other IRA men in the area, been on the run. Only Eily and Katherine, the Murphy daughters, shared their parents' house now.

The absent boys were a constant source of worry to the whole family. Under martial law the military were free to fight their enemies as they saw fit, and they had the local IRA run ragged. There were constant army patrols and sweeps of the countryside, and an endless stream of arrests of both guilty and innocent. Now and again some of the rebels would be caught where they couldn't retreat, and would decide to fight it out. When they did that they lost, usually with several dead or wounded before they surrendered. The heavy army presence in the towns kept them cut off from most of their supplies, and their sympathisers in the countryside were gradually being arrested or frightened into cooperation with the authorities or at least non-cooperation with the Volunteers. Even safe houses were no longer safe: three farms had been burned as reprisals for attempted ambushes, and though the ambushes hadn't stopped altogether after that, still, they'd tailed off dramatically – though mainly because the Volunteers had hardly enough ammunition to defend themselves if they had to, never mind mount an ambush.

In the town, meanwhile, there were soldiers everywhere, and a strict night-time curfew. Hardly a day passed without at least one army raid on the house of suspected rebel sympathisers. Eddie and Myles were known to be 'out', and the authorities kept a close eye on the whole Murphy family.

There had been half a dozen raids on the house in the past couple of months, mainly in the middle of the night, and that hadn't done Mr Murphy's heart – or his temper – much good at all. He'd liked his night's sleep, had Mr Murphy, especially when he had a sup taken. It wouldn't have been so bad if he'd been a rebel himself, but he'd always thought his sons were daft to get involved with the IRA at all. They'd had terrible arguments about it in the past, before the boys went on the run.

'Youse might as well be out there playing gouts,' he used to say to Myles and Eddie. 'Youse might as well be playing cowboys for all the differ youse will make to the British army. Them boyos bet the Boers and they bet the Germans, and the Boers and the Germans were better soldiers nor your crowd will ever be. All youse will do is bring trouble on your own. And even if youse *did* beat them, what would happen? Who'd take over then? Every jumped-up gombeen man in Ireland would put on a morning coat and queue up to get to the trough, and the bishops would be standing over them, grinning, blessing them on their way.'

Myles, his eldest son, knew better than to get into a row with his father, but Eddie, who was only nineteen, was a hothead, and would always make the mistake of answering his father back.

'Our republic will be for all Irishmen,' he'd say angrily. 'And if the clergy don't know their place then they'll be taught it. The bishops are no friends of ours.'

But his father would just laugh at talk like that, while his mother would chastise Eddie for speaking disrespectfully of the Church. It was hard to know which annoyed Eddie more, his Da laughing at him or his Ma giving out to him like he was a child. He'd stand fuming for a while, redfaced and speechless, and then he'd storm out of the house; but in a few days or weeks the very same routine would be repeated, and Eddie would rise to the bait yet again.

Such entertainment had been gone, of course, since the lads went on the run, and Mrs Murphy had even been known to say she missed the rows; certainly they'd upset Eddie, but at least he'd been there to be upset. Now she never knew when she might hear he was dead in a ditch somewhere. And she'd never heard her husband laugh as much as he did at Eddie's political views, not since the time the ratty old fleabag of a lion in the travelling show had attacked its handler, not long after the Murphys were married. Since the boys went on the run the only excitement in the house had been the army raids, and Mr Murphy hadn't found them one bit funny. He hadn't been afraid of the soldiers, who in any case always seemed more embarrassed than anything else to be disturbing plainly harmless people in the middle of the night; but it was annoying to be rousted out of your sleep and to stand around in your nightshirt with your family while total strangers searched your house.

'What are youse looking for, anyhow?' Mr Murphy would demand of their officer. 'Do youse think I have room to hide two big strapping buckos of lads in a house the size of this? My boys are not midgets, you know. It's not the seven dwarves youse are fighting.'

The officer – it was usually Captain Cobbett, a terribly nice young man who was always very respectful and apologetic – would hem and haw and make reassuring noises, which is quite hard to do, really, when your men are tramping all over someone's house in their big army boots, prodding bayonets into all sorts of unlikely corners. None of the young officers liked raiding the Murphys. It was well known around the town that Mr Murphy, though certainly no flaming loyalist, thought very little of the rebels, and was unlikely to be harbouring them or hiding material for their use. But his sons were well-known Volunteers, and known to be on the run, so raids on their home were automatically ordered from headquarters. Even if nothing was found, the theory ran, it would make the Murphys dislike the IRA even more. In practice, of course, it made Mr Murphy dislike the army just as much as he disliked the IRA.

'They're all the same,' he used to say to whoever would listen when the subject came up. 'A load of young chaps running around with too many guns. The army was never the same since they left off the red coats, anyhow. The best of them died in the war. These are all amateurs now, on the two sides. Only chaps, the whole lot of them.'

Mr Murphy spoke of military matters with an air of some authority, based on the fact that he'd once had a cousin in the ranks. His own military experience was non-existent, barring what he read in the papers. But even he could see that those ordering the midnight raids had a very poor grasp of civilian psychology.

'A few more of these raids,' he'd told Captain Cobbett one night, 'and I'll start running guns just to spite you. I'll have a party for the boys and invite every gunman in Leinster. I'll hide pikes in the rafters, and dynamite in the shoe-polish tin, and bullets in the butter-dish.'

'Now now, Mr Murphy,' Captain Cobbett said. 'There's no need to take that attitude. These are difficult times for everyone.'

'I don't care about "everyone",' Mr Murphy said, 'any more than "everyone" cares about me. I cares about me and mine. Sure, I can hardly close my eyes at night for wondering whether youse are going to start banging on the door as soon as I go asleep. Me poor wife's nerves are in flitters, and youse have the fear of God put into them two young ones there.'

The two 'young ones', Katherine and Eily, always seemed to Captain Cobbett to be anything but afraid. While Mrs Murphy was torn between admiration for her boys' spirit and fear for their lives, her daughters had no such qualms. In their own way they were as bad as their brothers. Katherine, who was sixteen, at least had the sense to stay quiet while the house was being raided, although there were daggers in her eyes whenever she looked at the soldiers. Eily, who was thirteen, didn't even have that much patience. She was an out-and-out rebel sympathiser, and complained loudly about every step a soldier took inside her house. As far as she was concerned, she told them quite frankly, there were only two good places for a British soldier to be: in his own home or dead.

'Haven't youse a big enough empire?' she'd demand of them. 'Go and annoy a few natives out foreign someplace, why don't you? What do youse want to bother us for?'

When she said things like that you could see her parents cringe, but almost all of the soldiers saw the girl's fury as a good joke. Among themselves they called her a fiery little thing, and they said it almost with admiration. During a raid they would smile at her high spirits, until their sergeant had to tell them to take their job seriously. Just as her father's laughter used to aggravate Eddie, so the soldiers' smiles only made Eily angrier. She'd stand there brazenly in her nightdress with her face glowing redder and redder, with Katherine and her mother restraining her lest she physically attack some of the foreign young men. It wasn't funny, really. Captain Cobbett had even gone so far as to warn Mr Murphy to be careful.

'That's a hotheaded young lady you have there, sir,' he'd told the old man once. 'She's very free with seditious comments. It's all right her saying those sort of things around us – I mean, she's only a kid, and I can even under-stand her point of view. I wouldn't want soldiers tramping around my house either. Fortunately my own men rather like the child. But I don't think the Black and Tans would take her carry-on very well, if you know what I mean. They're not great men for humour, the Tans.'

That was putting it mildly. The Black and Tans would burn the Murphys' house down around their ears if Eily were to say to them half the things she said to the young soldiers. And she wasn't even content to keep her treason within her own four walls. When she went out she wore a tricoloured ribbon around her hat to symbolise her sup-port for the rebels. Mr Murphy had lost count of the number of times he'd torn off the ribbon, but she'd always found another somewhere. The sight of her walking down the street with the ends of the green, white and orange ribbon waving gaily in the air behind her gave him, Mr Murphy used to say, the palpitations. And of course no-one had taken that seriously either, when he said it. But there he was now, stretched out dead in the parlour, with his palpitations as far behind him as his arguments with Eddie and Eily. He, at least, had no more worries.

*　　*　　*

The funeral was next day. What with the curfew, of course, there was no question of having a proper wake; but the family sat up with the body anyway, and during the evening a few neighbours dropped by to offer condolences and remark on how well the corpse looked. Nellie Browne stayed after the others had gone. She lived in the next house in the terrace, so she didn't bother about the curfew, what with the night that was in it. Katherine and Eily wanted to sit with their mother awhile too, but Mrs Murphy made them go to bed. Then she and Nellie sat up talking by the dying fire. The oil-lamp stood on the mantelpiece, and six white candles burned around the coffin in candlesticks loaned by the undertaker. Mrs Murphy threw a bit of coal and few sods of turf on the embers of the fire, and turned the big wheel bellows to redden them. Sugrue, the cat, sat between them and looked into the glowing coals, communing with the fire.

'Every time I turns this wheel,' Mrs Murphy said, 'I thinks of poor Jack doing it when the lads were small. He used to have an ould rhyme that he'd say for them when he was doing it, and they only babbies: *"Jeremiah, blow the fire. Puff! Puff! Puff! First he blows it gentle, and then he blows it rough."*'

She cast her eye over to where her husband lay now, his eyes closed under the two copper pennies, his grey hair sleeked flat with macassar oil, a rosary beads clasped in his cold, joined hands.

'He was full of ould notions and sayings,' she said. 'And he drank too much sometimes. But he was a good man – a good husband. And he doted on them childer.'

'He wasn't sick long,' Nellie said. 'There's that at least, ma'am.'

The new widow agreed with Nellie: a long illness would have been worse.

'Though a short one would have been nice,' she said. 'I'd've liked a *little* bit of a warning. Just so I could say goodbye, like.'

She sighed. 'It's a cruel cross I have to carry now, all the same,' she said. 'Me man gone, and me two boys hunted across the country like wild animals, not even knowing their own father is dead – though they might be dead themselves for all I know.'

She shook her head.

'I don't know how I'm going to manage,' she said.

'Not wanting to be nosey, ma'am,' Nellie said, 'but had he no savings or anything?'

Mrs Murphy, in spite of her loss, couldn't restrain a polite guffaw.

'Savings?' she said. 'Our Jack? No more nor what'll bury him. But we should be all right for a few shillings, as far as that goes. Meself and Katherine and Eily all does the bit of sewing, and it brings the money in in dribs and drabs.'

'Better dribs and drabs, ma'am, nor not at all,' Nellie said.

'True for you, Mrs Browne,' Mrs Murphy said. 'But 'tis not the money that worries me, 'tis the childer. Especially young Eily.'

'Eily is a wild one, right enough,' Nellie said. 'Could Jack manage her, then?'

This time Mrs Murphy managed not to laugh out loud.

'He surely couldn't,' she said. 'She had him heartscalded with the worry. Sure there's no managing with her. She's that wilful you wouldn't believe it. Do you know, this very morning I sent her down to Crimmins's, the undertakers, to have someone come up and lay poor Jack out here in his coffin. "*Go straight there*," I told her, "*and come straight back*." And wasn't she gone for two hours, and when she came back she told me she didn't go to Crimmins's at all! "*I went to Morans*'," says she. "*He's a good republican undertaker. His son is on the run with Myles and Eddie, and he'll be proud to do his best job for the father of two warriors of the republic.*"'

Nellie gasped. 'Lord between us and all harm!' she said. 'The cheek of it! I'd redden the poker for her, if she was mine. And her poor father lying there dead! If our Mary did anything like that she'd get the back of my hand!'

'The worst of it was,' Mrs Murphy said, 'that she was right. Ould Moran himself come up, with two of his men. They brought in big boxes of undertakers' stuff, and they were working on him there for an hour and more. They sent us all out to the kitchen till they were done, and when we come back there was Jack, the very way you see him now. And do you know, ould Moran said he wouldn't take a shilling off me for the work. "*It's the very least we can do for the man,*" says he.'

'Still, she had no business going for him at all,' Nellie said. 'And childer have no business being right – it's not natural. I'd have taken a stick to her if I were you.'

'It's too late for that with Eily,' Mrs Murphy said. 'She'd probably throw something at me if I raised my hand to her. Her father had her ruined – had them all ruined, for that matter. Jack was dead set against hitting childer. "*It's only bullying them,*" he used to say. I even got Father Owens to talk to him about it one time, because I was afraid it might be a sin not to hit them. Father Owens told Jack it was a parent's duty to chastise their childer. It was in the Bible, he said. But me bould Jack would have none of it. "'*Tis a queer class of a God would condemn me all the same, Father,*" says he, "*for not beating them as is smaller and weaker nor me.*" And he started quoting the Bible right back at Father Owens, like a Protestant or a Freethinker.'

'Quoting the *Bible*?' said Nellie, crossing herself quickly.

'Oh aye – chapter and verse. Of course, that was the end of that – you knows the way priests hates that kind of carry on.'

Again she looked over at the corpse in the open coffin. But there was fondness in the look.

'Twenty-five year we were married,' she said, 'and he never stopped surprising me in all that time. 'Tisn't every-one can say that.'

'Indeed 'tis not,' Nellie said, sounding vaguely shocked. 'Our Tom stopped surprising me years before we were ever married,' she said proudly.

They were both still sitting, silently contemplating the general unsurprisingness of men, when the great banging started at the door. Sugrue jumped only slightly more than the two women.

'Open up!' called a loud male voice. 'Open up in there!'

'Sacred Heart!' said Mrs Murphy. 'They'd never raid us on a night like tonight! God forgive them!'

Nellie hurried to the window and looked out. 'Oh Lord,' she said, 'but it's them, right enough.'

Katherine and Eily appeared in their nightclothes on the stairs.

'They wouldn't!' Katherine said. 'They couldn't!'

The pounding on the door continued.

'Open the door, Ma,' Eily said. 'Before they knocks it down.'

Mrs Murphy went to the front door and unbarred it. When she opened the door she saw soldiers crowding round in the street outside. Captain Cobbett stood in the front. He looked mortified.

'Mrs Murphy, ma'am,' he said. 'Please accept my apologies …'

Mrs Murphy was a quiet woman, but this was too much.

'May God forgive you, Captain Cobbett!' she said. 'Have youse no respect for anything at all? My man is dead in the room inside, laid out for the grave. You knows there's nothing here.'

The captain looked totally shamefaced.

'I know, ma'am,' he said. 'I pointed that out to my superiors. But somebody told them your boys would come in by the back lanes tonight to see their father for a last time.'

'Well, they didn't,' Mrs Murphy said. Her voice was black with anger. 'My lads is out on the mountains. They don't even know that their daddy is dead. Captain Cobbett, have you no pity? Have you no respect even for the dead?'

The young captain squirmed.

'This is not my doing, Mrs Murphy,' he said. 'Believe me, this is the last place on earth I want to be. But I'm a soldier, and I have my orders. I have no choice in the matter. We'll be as quick as we can.'

For a moment Mrs Murphy stood holding the door, as though to bar their way. But she knew it was useless. She flung the door wide and walked back in ahead of them. Behind her an NCO called: 'Move sharp now, lads. These people have enough on their plates. And for God's sake don't *break* anything!'

In the room, Nellie Browne still stood by the window. Eily and Katherine had taken the chairs by the fire. Eily sat with her head high and glared at the soldiers but, much to Mrs Murphy's surprise, she said nothing at all. Mrs Murphy had half-expected her to start cursing them the moment they walked in. Eily had been strangely quiet all day, in fact, ever since coming back from Morans'. In the kitchen, while they waited for Moran and his men to finish with Mr Murphy, she'd stood silent for ages looking up the back yard while Mrs Murphy and Katherine talked. Beyond the back wall lay the lanes, and beyond them the open country and the mountains. Mrs Murphy had wondered whether Eily, like herself, was thinking of Myles and Eddie, half-orphaned without even knowing it. Maybe her father's sudden death would have some kind of calming influence on her wildness. Mrs Murphy prayed that it would.

Sugrue had climbed into Eily's lap, and Eily was rubbing the old tom's head absentmindedly. The cat, unused to such attention, purred ravenously. Katherine sat staring deliberately into the fire, refusing even to look at the intruders. The soldiers – there must have been a dozen of them, and they all looked terribly young – filled the room. None seemed too anxious to go near the coffin, though all of them glanced at it fearfully and a couple, obviously Catholic, quickly crossed themselves. Someone lifted the latch on the back door, and more soldiers came in from the yard.

Captain Cobbett stood, embarrassed, in the middle of the room while his NCO directed the boys in khaki to the various rooms. Rough army boots rumbled on the narrow stairs. Cobbett's eyes moved around the room, avoiding Mrs Murphy's. But she wasn't going to let him ignore her. She stood foursquare in front of him, her arms akimbo, and said nothing until common politeness – of which the young officer had a great deal – forced him to look at her. Captain Cobbett was a tall man, and Mrs Murphy was a small woman, but there was no doubt who was intimidated by whom. Cobbett's face was russet with shame and embarrassment. As their eyes met, he seemed to flinch.

'Captain Cobbett,' Mrs Murphy said. 'This is too much. There's that man dead there in front of you, and never by word or deed did he do a single thing to you or to your army or your country. My sons are rebels. Even my daughters are half-rebels. But there was never a hand's turn done against you in this house. Your men have raided us a dozen times if they've done it once, and kept us standing here while you went through the place looking for sedition. But never a bullet or a gun have you found here. No secret letters, and no rebel orders, and no rebel supplies. Not so much as a pair of rebel boots have you found under my roof. And here you are again, and my poor husband stark dead in his coffin in front of you, and your men upstairs going through our few belongings. God forgive you, Captain Cobbett! You'll have no luck from this out. What are my daughters to think of your great British law and your great British justice? Is it any wonder that half of the young people are rebels? Youse are turning them against yourselves, so you are, with this kind of carry on.'

Cobbett met her fury as best he could.

'Mrs Murphy, ma'am,' he said, 'you're telling me

nothing that I didn't tell my superior officer myself earlier tonight. This is foolishness – I know it. Your husband was a good man, and no rebel. But you have to admit –'

'What?' she demanded. 'What do I have to admit? That my sons brought this on us? Is that what you were going to say? It isn't my sons clodhopping around my house leaving muck on my clean floors, Captain Cobbett. It isn't my sons rooting through our few poor things up above in the press, or terrifying my girls in the middle of the night.'

Sorry though he was, Captain Cobbett couldn't help reflecting that her girls didn't look very terrified. The young one in particular, Eily, glared at him with a look that would have killed him if it could.

'I'm here tonight, ma'am,' he said, 'because I was ordered to be here. And I frankly admit to you that I didn't agree with those orders. Neither you nor your husband has done anything to deserve this treatment. But these are troubled times – that's what I was going to say. You must admit that.'

Mrs Murphy barked a short, bitter laugh. 'Troubled times?' she said. 'My husband is dead. My sons hunted. I've soldiers all over my house. I don't need you to tell me about trouble, Captain.'

'No,' Cobbett said. 'I don't suppose you do.'

He looked over at his sergeant, who was standing, ramrod-stiff, at the bottom of the steep little stairs.

'Call them off, Sergeant Platt,' he said. 'We were told to

come, and we came. Now we can go.'

The sergeant obeyed with obvious gratitude, summoning the soldiers with a barked command. Nellie Browne stirred from her place by the window.

'I'll go now too, ma'am,' she said to Mrs Murphy. 'If the officer will allow.'

Cobbett, still red-faced, nodded curtly.

'Do you need an escort, madam?' he asked.

Nellie looked horrified at the thought.

'Oh no, sir,' she said. 'Sure, I'm only next door. But your men, sir,' she said, 'they won't shoot me or anything, will they? Or arrest me? Only, it's after the curfew hour.'

Cobbett sighed.

'Nobody is going to shoot anybody,' he said. 'We're just going to leave these people in what little peace they have.'

Nellie thanked him.

'I'll be in to you first thing in the morning,' she said to Mrs Murphy.

Again the soldiers' boots thundered as they hurried towards the front door. Nellie Browne let them go first. As she did there was a little moan, and Mrs Murphy collapsed. She would have fallen to the floor if Captain Cobbett hadn't caught her in his arms. Katherine and Eily were on their feet immediately.

'Mammy!' Katherine called.

'She's fainted,' Cobbett said. He stood awkwardly, holding the little woman in his arms like a straw doll.

'You made her faint, you mean!' Eily said. 'Hadn't she enough trouble on her plate without you bringing this down on top of her?'

'Shut up, Eily,' Kathleen said sharply, 'and get a wet tea towel at the sink. Wipe her face with it, and bring her around.'

Eily went, but Mrs Murphy was already starting to come round under her own steam. She stood, weakly, holding on to Cobbett's arm. By now Cobbett was furious as well as embarrassed. It wasn't anger at anyone here, though; it was anger at having been forced to trouble these people at such a time. If he ignored Eily's accusation, it was only because he believed she was perfectly right.

'You say you live next door, ma'am?' he asked Nellie Browne.

Nellie said she did.

'Will you take this lady out of this?' Cobbett asked. 'Take her where she'll have something else to look at apart from her dead husband, even for a little while. Sit her by your fire and give her a cup of tea, until she's recovered from our rudeness.'

'To be sure, sir, I will, and welcome,' Nellie said. 'If she'll go.'

Mrs Murphy by now was standing on her own two feet.

'I should stay here,' she said. 'I should stay with my man. It was only a little weakness.'

'Please, ma'am,' Cobbett said. 'I know our coming was

the final straw, but you've been under terrible pressure.'

'And who applied the pressure, if not yourselves?' sneered Eily, who'd come back with the tea towel.

Everyone ignored her. The soldiers, apart from Cobbett and the sergeant, were all outside. Eily went back to her chair and took Sugrue back on her lap. She laid the wet cloth on the hearth by the fire, where it started to steam.

Mrs Murphy's face looked drawn.

'Go ahead, Ma,' Katherine said. 'Even for the length of time it will take to drink a cup of tea. Myself and Eily will be grand. At least we're finished with the army for the night.'

'I can assure you of that much, anyway,' Cobbett said.

Mrs Murphy considered. You could see that, though she felt she shouldn't leave her husband on this last night, the idea of a few minutes by Nellie Browne's fire attracted her. Eily was stroking Sugrue again, fuming silently. The sergeant, tense, looked at Eily as she stroked the cat almost violently. In an effort to be pleasant he called gently to the animal, and stretched out his own hand to pet it. Eily snatched Sugrue up into her arms. The tom, taken aback, gave an angry, startled cry. Eily turned her deadly glare on the sergeant.

'Don't you touch that beast,' she said. 'He'll scrawb the hand off you. This cat is a Sinn Féiner.'

'All right!' Mrs Murphy said suddenly. It was as though Eily's outburst had decided her. She went and got her shawl and wrapped it round her.

'You two go to bed,' she said to the girls. 'I'll take a cup of tea with Mrs Browne, and I'll be back within the hour. Leave the door on the latch.'

She went out without another word. Nellie Browne hurried after her. Captain Cobbett went over and looked into the coffin. He took off his cap and stood briefly contemplating Jack Murphy's healthy, peaceful face. He turned to the two girls by the fire.

'I know you're angry with me,' he said. 'And I understand it. I'd be angry too, if I were in your place. But I hope you believe me that I don't like this one bit. My Colonel said your brothers would be here tonight. He said his information was from a reliable source.'

'I'll bet you I know who that source was, too,' Eily said. 'Ould Batty Crimmins, the undertaker, annoyed that he wasn't getting our business. That ould gombeen man would rob the coins off a dead man's eyes, so he would. How much did your Colonel pay him for his reliable information?'

Cobbett stared at her, startled. So much for the Colonel's confidence in his informant's discretion. Cobbett almost smiled. He quite looked forward to informing the Colonel that the very children of the town knew the identity of his most valued spy.

'I don't know what you're talking about,' he said to Eily, who smiled.

Katherine, who'd hardly looked at any of the soldiers

since they came in, stood up and turned to Cobbett.

'Would you just go, please?' she said. 'Just go, and leave us here with our dead.'

Cobbett nodded. 'Yes,' he said. 'I do believe that would be best.'

Neither girl said anything to that. Cobbett left without saying another word. The sergeant followed gratefully. In the street, back in their own world, they called orders to their men. The soldiers had crept up on the house quietly; they marched away in step, the sound of their boots fading into the night.

*　　*　　*

For a little while Eily and Katherine sat looking at each other warily. Sugrue had disappeared out the front door with the soldiers.

'Well,' Eily said finally. 'I was afraid there for a minute. But it came out even better than I hoped.'

'No thanks to you,' Katherine said tartly. 'You'll have to learn to mind your temper, Eily Murphy. Or at least your mouth. You could have ruined us all if you'd annoyed them soldiers.'

'Well, I didn't,' Eily said. 'And they're gone. And even Nellie and Ma are gone.'

Katherine went to the window and pulled a corner of the curtain aside.

'I hope they're gone anyway,' she said. 'You'd never know but they might have left a man in the yard.'

'They wouldn't dare,' Eily said dismissively. 'Poor Captain Cobbett was mortified.'

'He was,' Katherine said. 'I pitied him. The poor man was ashamed of his life!'

'So he should be,' Eily said. 'Intruding on our grief.'

She took the oil lamp from the mantelpiece and went into the back kitchen. The parlour darkened but for the glow of the candles and the fire. Katherine stood by the window and looked down at her dead father's face.

'I'm sorry to use you this way, Daddy,' she said very softly to the dead man. 'But these are desperate times. I done it for Eddie and Myles. I know you'll forgive me, wherever you are.' She reached down and touched the cold hands crossed on his breast.

Eily came back into the room.

'There's no-one in the yard,' she said.

'Did you leave the lamp in the window?'

'I did, with the wick low.'

'Well,' Katherine said, 'there's nothing to do now only wait.'

But they didn't have to wait. They heard the latch on the back door almost immediately, and, for the second time that night, the sound of men's boots in the back kitchen. The three men who came into the room brought the smell of the cold night and the fields with them. They were done up in caps and greatcoats and hung about with belts and bandoliers. Each of them carried an empty sack, and all three had empty canvas knapsacks on their backs and rifles on slings over their shoulders.

Eily ran and threw her arms around the first of the men.

'Myles!' she said. 'Thank God!'

Her big brother clasped her to him, but then pushed her gently aside and went over to the coffin. He took off his cap and stared down at his father in silence. Katherine, studying Myles's grim face, thought he looked like a stranger. He was like a man in his forties, who hadn't laughed in at least twenty years. But she knew he was only twenty-two. She glanced at the other two men. One was Simon Moran, the undertaker's son. The other was a stranger. They seemed every bit as grim.

'Is Eddie all right?' she asked Myles.

Her brother looked at her.

'He's grand,' he said. 'But he couldn't come. He's off on a bit of business.'

He gestured towards the coffin.

'Was he long sick?' he asked. 'I heard nothing.'

'There was no warning,' Eily told him. 'He died in his sleep in the night. There was a raid tonight, Myles, and he lying there dead. Just now. They're gone.'

'And Mammy?'

'Next door in Nellie Browne's for a while. She'll be back in a bit if you want to see her.'

'No,' Myles said. 'It's better this way. I'd love to see her, but she wouldn't understand.'

'Do you think *he'd* understand?' Katherine asked, nodding at the man in the coffin.

To her surprise, her big brother actually grinned. It took twenty years off him, and made him look like himself.

'Do you know,' he said, 'I think Da might find the whole thing very funny.'

'He would if it was happening to someone else,' Eily said. 'But not to himself.'

'Aye,' Myles said. 'Maybe so.'

'Ma wouldn't find it funny at all,' Katherine said. 'That's for sure. And I don't find it very funny meself, either.'

'No,' Myles said. 'But what's done is done. We'd best get finished now before Ma comes back.'

He put his rifle and the sack he carried on the floor, and took off the empty knapsack. Then he turned to the other two men.

'Are you still on for it?' he asked.

'Needs must,' Simon Moran said.

The third man was looking nervously at the corpse.

'You're the poor man's son, Myles,' he said. 'If you're on for it, then I am.'

The others also laid down their rifles and sacks and took off their bags. Then all three gathered round the coffin. They blessed themselves and said a quick, nervous prayer. Then Myles Murphy took hold of his dead father's shoulders, and Simon Moran took his feet. The third man took a half-hearted grip of the dead man's hips. They hauled.

'The pennies!' Simon Moran hissed at Katherine. 'They'll fall! Take them up!'

Katherine reached out to take the pennies off her father's eyes. Her hand stopped a couple of inches from his face. She couldn't. Eily pushed her aside.

'Get out of that!' she said to her sister. 'It's too late now to be squeamish.'

She picked the two red pennies off the eyes without hesitation. Katherine felt a rush of relief when she saw the eyes remained shut. She hadn't wanted them looking at her, accusing her.

'Lift now, boys,' Myles said. He was gritting his teeth. The stranger nervously touched the cloth of Mr Murphy's grey trousers. Simon Moran showed no trace of any feeling at all. He was used to such work, Katherine supposed – he was an undertaker's son, after all.

'He's as stiff as a board!' the third man said. And he was. The body didn't bend at all as the men lifted it out and put it, with an apologetic air, on the floor. Katherine looked at it there and felt ashamed. But Simon Moran had been right: needs must.

The coffin was lined with a shiny black cloth. With a single, expert gesture, Simon Moran whipped the cloth out. The coffin lay bared, but not at all empty. The bottom was lined with a tightly-packed layer of packets and boxes. Myles lifted one small, heavy carton and took the lid off. The box was packed with neat rows of pointy-headed bullets.

'Lee-Enfield ammo,' he said. 'The very thing. Right, now, lads. Fill your bags.'

The three of them fell on the contents of the coffin, loading the boxes and packets into the sacks and canvas bags. Simon Moran sniffed at one big, solid parcel that was wrapped in butcher's paper. He untied the string around it and peeped inside.

'A ham!' he said exultantly. 'A whole ham! It feels like a lifetime since I saw anything like this!'

Katherine was still looking at the little dead man on the floor. There were a whole lot of things now, she thought, that seemed like a lifetime ago.

When the coffin was emptied of its treasures Simon Moran put the lining back in. Then the three of them picked Mr Murphy up off the floor and placed him back in his box.

'He's lower in that box now nor he was before,' the third man said. 'Somebody will notice.'

Myles looked around the room. The lid of the coffin stood against the wall in the corner.

'Put the top on,' he said. He looked at Eily. 'You tell Ma that you got afraid looking at him,' he said. 'Say you and Katherine covered him up.'

Katherine, for all her low mood, almost laughed.

'Eily?' she said. 'Afraid? Sure nobody would believe that. I'll say it was me got afraid.'

She looked at her father in the box. Eily had put the two

pennies back on her father's eyes, but still Katherine seemed to feel him looking at her.

'It will be only half a lie anyway,' she said.

The men laid the lid loosely on the coffin. In the flickering light of the candles they uncovered their heads and stood and said a little prayer. Then they picked up their now-bulging bags and their rifles.

'We won't linger,' Myles said. 'Say nothing to Ma. She've enough on her mind.'

Eily threw herself on him again. She held on to him as though she'd never let go.

'Mind yourself,' she said. 'And mind Eddie.'

'I will,' Myles said. 'And I'll be far better able to do the two things with all this stuff. You're great girls, the pair of you.'

'Aye,' Katherine said. She was still looking at the coffin. 'Great girls entirely.'

Myles put his hand on her shoulder.

'You mind Eily,' he said. 'Don't let her get herself in trouble.'

Then he took Eily's arms from around his neck, and the three men left without looking back. Eily followed them to the back door. She stood in the doorway watching them go up the back yard in the moonlight until they disappeared in the darkness. Then she shut the door and took the oil-lamp and raised the wick and carried the lamp into the front room. Katherine was back sitting by the fire, staring into the flames. Eily put the lamp on the mantelpiece and sat down in the other chair across from her. In her triumph she'd almost forgotten the fact that her father was dead.

'Well,' she said. 'That went well.'

Katherine looked up at her.

'Aye,' she said. 'I suppose it did.'

The light shone on tears on her face. Eily was going to say something, but thought better of it. They sat there for a few minutes in silence. Then they heard the latch open on the front door, and their mother's slow, shuffling footsteps coming into the hall.

The Poor Cow

You should always tell your Mam where you're going. One time when I was young I didn't do that, and because of it a lot of people died. It destroyed our lives entirely. And it was only an ordinary day, and I was only trying to help. But the times weren't ordinary, do you see; though that wasn't my fault.

I was in the kitchen that day. I suppose it was around two o'clock. I happened to look out the window and I saw the Tans going through the yard. My mother was foostering around dusting everything, whether it was dusty or not, the way that she did when she'd nothing else to keep her busy. She was a great one for the dusting, my mother. She'd nearly dust the dinner, my father used to say.

'Mam,' I said, soft like, when I saw the Tans. 'Look in the yard.'

She glanced out the window and nearly dropped the cloth she was dusting with.

'Jesus, Mary and Joseph!' she said. 'Are they coming here?'

A few of the Tans looked towards the house, but they didn't stop. One of them, bringing up the rear, saw me through the window. I remember he had a very handsome face. He gave an ugly little smile when he saw me, and pointed his rifle at me through the window as he passed. For a moment I was looking at him down the gun's barrel. Then my mother pulled me away from the window and stood holding me to her. I could feel her heart beating as fast as my own. We listened, but after a while we realised the Tans had just been passing. You wouldn't miss the Tans' knock on your door – if they bothered to knock, instead of just kicking it in.

'Mother of god,' my mother said, 'even the sight of them blackguards would make you weak. What are they doing round here? It's not often you'd see them so far from their lorries.'

From the way that the Tans had been going, they must have come through the fields. I knew there'd been an ambush on the Lackduffane road the day before. The Tans had beaten it off, wounding some of their attackers. I guessed now they were hunting for them, hoping to find the wounded at least. I said as much to my mother.

'Well, they won't find them here,' she said. 'Nor a welcome themselves if they call. There'll be no sort of gunmen under my roof if I can help it.'

It was another little while before either of us thought of Hannah. Hannah was the cow. She'd been out in the near field since morning, and if the Tans had come across the fields they must have passed through there to get into the yard. I knew they hadn't shot her, as they'd been known to do with cattle sometimes, because we'd have heard the shot. But I'd been told of a case where they'd cut the throats of some cattle, wanting to kill them but ordered by their officers not to waste bullets. That was a kind of wantonness farm people simply couldn't understand. That was pure badness and spite.

The near field was round by the back corner of the house, out of sight of any window. To check on Hannah meant going outside. I wanted to go straight away, but my Mam didn't want me to go at all.

'Them Tans are long gone now,' I said.

She was still nervous, but she was worried about Hannah too.

'All right,' she said. 'But come straight back.'

There were two gates in the near field. One led into the yard, the other one out to the lane. I saw straight away that the Tans had left the yard gate open, but that was all right: we'd have seen Hannah if she'd come into the yard. But when I got to the near field I saw that the gate to the lane was open too, and the field was empty. The Tans hadn't killed Hannah; but they'd let her stray.

'Boy!'

I jumped at the sound of the single word. When I looked round I saw Tans coming through the hedge from the next field. Like the ones who'd gone through our yard, they were dressed in RIC uniforms. The Tans were gradually being kitted out with proper police clothing, but you could always tell them at a glance, even before they spoke and you heard their foreign accents. The real RIC were all fine figures of men, bigger and taller than almost all the Tans. Even dressed in police uniforms the Tans looked like impostors.

They were breaking the hedge as they came, making it useless. My father would have to repair that, I thought. As if he hadn't enough to do. These Tans were supposed to be the police; but they did more damage than any criminals. They seemed to have a lot of meanness in them.

The man who'd called me was an officer with a little moustache on his lip and a big revolver in his hand. He beckoned me over and I went. He looked me up and down.

'What are you doing here, boy?' he asked me.

I pointed at the house. 'I lives over there, sir,' I said.

He looked where I pointed.

'Seen any strangers around here, have you?' he asked.

'Only some of your own men, sir. They went through our yard around ten minutes ago.'

'Which way did they go?'

'They just passed through, sir. They looked like they were making for the hills above, but I didn't see what way they went.'

He said a curse.

'They can't follow the simplest instruction,' he said. Then he looked away and forgot about me, and shouted at his men to come on. He led them through the gate into our yard. I stood looking after them but heard nothing that suggested trouble, so I thought about Hannah again.

When all was said and done I'd have to go after her. I might as well go now. Hannah had a head start on me, but she'd hardly be gone very far. I should have told my Mam what I was doing, I know. Everything would have been all right if I'd only done that. But I was too taken up with thinking of Hannah. She was the only cow we had left.

I didn't want to wait till the Tans had cleared out of the yard, and then go in and persuade my Mam to let me go. That would only give Hannah an even bigger head start – if Mam let me go at all. She'd be worried with Tans on the loose. They were unpredictable men, which was exactly why I wanted Hannah back as soon as possible. So I made for the gate to the lane.

Hannah was a hungry cow. I'd hoped maybe she'd stopped in the lane to eat the grass there. Everything would have been grand if she'd only done that. But there was no sign of her, barring a trail of fresh cowdung that showed the way she'd gone – down the lane towards the main road. So I set off after her. It was a rambling sort of a lane, twisting along between the odd-shaped fields, and every time I rounded a bend I hoped to see Hannah there browsing. But I walked on a good bit and all I saw was the dung.

It was a fine day. I pulled a switch off a bare hazel tree in the ditch for when I'd meet Hannah. She was a contrary beast, and needed more driving than most. But with every step that I went I was getting more annoyed, and I knew I'd be only too happy to beat her home today. I'd get in trouble when I got back. I was sorry now I hadn't told Mam where I was going. She'd take the head off me when I got home.

I was turning one bend in the lane when I met Biddy Wall. The Walls' farm, like ours, was small, with scattered fields. A lot of the farms around our way were like that. Biddy, I knew, would be after leaving out their own few cows in a field that the Walls had round that way. She carried a switch like my own, and she was chopping at the nettles with it.

'Larry!' says Biddy. 'The very man. Is your Hannah after going astray?'

'She is, Biddy,' says I. 'There was Tans come through the yard and left the gate open.'

Biddy spat at the mention of the Tans. She was a great one for the spitting, Biddy was. She could a spit in a man's eye at five yards, they used to say.

'Well, I met Syl Sinnott beyant at the cross,' Biddy said, 'and he had a cow with him he didn't know. He was nearly after running into her on his ass and car. We thought it was Hannah, but we weren't sure. So I said when I was up this way I'd ask youse was she gone.'

The crossroads was at the very end of the lane, where it came out on the road. I wouldn't have thought Hannah was so far ahead of me. Maybe something had frightened her. Maybe the Tans had stampeded her out of pure devilment. They could have done a lot worse, but it was still an annoyance.

'And where is she now?' I asked Biddy.

'Syl said he'd bring her home to their own place,' she said. 'He'll put her in with their cows and you can collect her any time you like. I'd have brought her up meself only I wasn't sure it was her.'

I sighed. Sinnotts' farm was a lot further than I'd meant to go. But I was gone a good bit already. If I went home now I'd only have the whole distance to go over again, and all because my Mam worried too much.

Biddy half-read my mind.

'Cut across the fields to Sinnotts',' she said. 'You'll still have to bring her back by the road, but it'll save you a distance on the way there at least.'

'Aye,' I said. It would only be making the best of a bad job, but the job would have to be done sooner or later anyway.

I should at least have asked Biddy to go on to our house and tell Mam what I was at. But I never thought of it. Biddy would have suggested it herself if she'd known how things were. But it never struck either of us. I went in over the ditch at the next gap and headed cross-country towards

Sinnotts'. Biddy went back down the lane towards her home.

The fields were empty of people at that time of year, and I had a lonesome journey. I knew the afternoon was wearing on, and started to think that maybe this was all a bad idea. I dreaded the thought of having to drive Hannah home from Sinnotts' in the dark. I wasn't very superstitious, but it was said that old Mrs Mahon had heard the banshee keening three nights running that week. I didn't like the sound of that. And whatever about the banshee, there were the Tans to worry about.

Looking back on it now, my foolishness amazes me. Sinnotts' was miles away by road, and there was no way I'd ever have got Hannah back before night. The sensible thing would have been to collect her the next day. I knew she was safe, which should have been the important thing. I don't know what I was thinking of. Probably I wasn't thinking at all. That's often how bad things happen: not because somebody means to do ill but because they don't think about what they're doing at all.

But I meant well. I wanted to help. Our farm was failing, and my father had had to take a job at the bacon factory in the town. It had been a bitter thing for him, but he'd felt he had no choice. Every morning he'd saddle the big horse and ride off down the lane. He hated it; he was a farmer, and that was all he wanted. And he felt that the farm would just fail all the quicker without him there. Myself and my

Mam were left to run things at home, and I was desperate to prove I could manage. I hoped it would make my father feel better. Maybe that was what I was trying to do that day: prove that I could manage. In which case, looking back, I picked a stupid way to prove it.

My journey led me across fields big and small. The going was uphill most of the way, and I met only animals. It was mainly livestock farming around our way, with lately some root crops and cereals. I met many a cow in the fields as I went, and nervous sheep that shied away from me in their foolish way, bleating warnings at one another. Halligans' bull was in their upland field, left on his own there because of his famous temper. I gave him a wide berth, for he was a cross animal that liked no other creature on four legs or two. I imagined what would happen if a party of Tans tried to cross his field, and I smiled to myself. Then it struck me that they'd only kill him if he charged them, and I stopped smiling.

A bit beyond Halligan's field I came to the crest of the land and the richer ground fell away and lay before me. I saw the empty road below, and the fertile fields of the broad river valley. Sinnotts' roadside farmhouse looked lovely and snug just a mile or so ahead of me. It was a big, solid, single-storey thatched house, surrounded by various out-buildings. The Sinnotts had been there for a long time. They were prosperous. They had their own steam thresher and the latest in galvanised Dutch barns. A big apple orchard lay behind the house. In summer local children loved any excuse to call there, because old Mrs Sinnott, the mother, would never let a child go away without its pockets stuffed full of apples. Old Adam Sinnott, the father, was regarded as a lucky man. He and his wife had a brood of fine boys to help out on the farm. There were seven brothers, and the youngest, Matt, was in his twenties. He was a great friend of my father's, and was often up at our house. Old Adam must have been nearly seventy, but he was as strong as a man half his age. They were a well-liked and well-respected family, too pleasant even to envy.

As I started down the hill I saw men moving in a field to the east, maybe half a mile from Sinnotts' house. They were too far away for me to make out much about them, but I could see at least that they weren't in uniform. There were maybe half a dozen of them, and they were moving in single file by the ditch towards the house. I was looking at them when somebody called me by name, and I turned around.

It was Matt Sinnott who'd called me. He was coming over the ditch from the next field.

'Would you be here about a cow, be any chance, Lar?' he asked. I liked Matt. He was a laugh.

'Biddy Wall says your Syl found our Hannah,' I said.

Matt came over. 'Aye,' he said. 'He come in with her a while ago. He'd've brought her up only he had business back here. I'm surprised you came for her today, though.'

He nodded to where the sun was already well down in

the sky. In an hour or two it would be fully dark, and the heart sank in me when I imagined being out on the black, lonely road trying to drive a contrary cow. I'd been trying to keep thoughts of Tans and banshees from my mind as I came. In truth I'd only got this far because every step I took made it seem an even greater waste of time to turn back. But now that I'd arrived I cursed myself as a fool for ever coming.

'I should have waited till the morning,' I said. 'Only I wanted to make sure it was Hannah. I couldn't see how she'd got so far.'

'Oh it's Hannah, all right,' Matt said. 'She've the scar on her leg where the cur dog bit her that time.'

Matt would know her, all right. He'd often seen her up at our house.

'Where is she now?' I asked him.

'She's with our own beasts down by the house. It's not like you to let her stray.'

Matt always treated me like I knew what I was doing. It was something not all grown-ups did.

''Twasn't me let her out,' I said. ''Twas Tans come through our near field.'

'Tans?' said Matt, interested. 'What Tans?'

'There was two different loads of them come through our yard. The first lot left the lane gate open. I think they stampeded Hannah – she must have been running to get to the road so far ahead of me. I can't have been much more nor quarter of an hour behind her.'

But Matt was more interested in my news of Tans than in how Hannah had got out.

'Was there many of them?' he asked me.

I tried to think. I shrugged.

'Twenty or thirty altogether, I suppose,' I said.

'And what way were they headed?'

'I don't know. Towards the hills, I think. Away from here, anyhow.'

No-one liked to hear there were Black and Tans near their house, especially after an ambush. The Tans were unpredictable at the best of times, but after an ambush they got very dangerous. They liked to hit back at whoever was handiest to them. The Sinnotts might be prosperous, popular and respectable people, but to the Tans they were just natives, like the rest of us.

'Come down to the house,' Matt said. 'You must be hungry and thirsty after that walk. My mother will want to feed you.'

'I only want to start back, Matt,' I said. 'I was a fool to come at all.'

Matt threw back his head and laughed.

'If you think you'll escape my Ma's hospitality,' he said, 'then you're even more foolish.'

We made our way down the slope towards Sinnotts', approaching from the back. I'd forgotten about the men in the field. When I looked in that direction now I saw no-one. It had probably been the rest of the Sinnotts.

Sinnotts' farmyard had a dry stone wall around it that was as high as my chest. Old Adam one day had told me that, when he was about my own age, he'd helped his father put that wall up. I always remembered that. When he said it, it was the first time I'd ever really thought about an old man being young: about fathers being sons one time, and then becoming fathers and having sons of their own. It was a comfortable notion, a notion that spoke of things continuing. My own father worried that he'd have no farm to leave for me. Sinnotts didn't have such worries.

Now when we reached the barred metal gate in that stone wall Matt Sinnott put a hand out and stopped me.

'Just wait here for one second, will you, Larry?' he asked me, and I thought that was odd. The Sinnotts' house was always open to all. But I did as Matt asked – sure, why wouldn't I?

Matt made his way across the yard through a squawking mass of chickens. He went into the house and he was gone for a short while. I looked around, seeing would I maybe catch sight of Hannah. I thought again about the long road home in the dark.

Matt came back out. His brother Conor was with him, and another man I didn't know. The stranger was dressed in ordinary clothes, but over the legs of his trousers he wore leather leggings that reached to his knees.

'Come in, Larry, and welcome,' Conor said. 'And tell us about these Black and Tans.'

I told him the little I knew as we went inside. Conor and the stranger exchanged looks I couldn't read.

'You say they were heading up into the hills?' the stranger said. He was a thin-faced man with sharp eyes.

'I thought they were. The first lot looked to be headed that way. But the officer with the second lot got annoyed when I told him that. I don't think they were supposed to go up there.'

Again Conor and the stranger looked at each other.

'How long ago did this happen?' the stranger asked.

I looked at the big clock Sinnotts had in their kitchen. It was half-past four.

I tried to think what time I'd seen the Tans.

''Twasn't long after two,' I said.

The stranger ran a hand through his hair, thinking.

'They're out hunting anyhow,' he said. 'We'd maybe better move.'

'What about the hurted lads?' Conor said.

I tried not to look too curious, but an odd and frightening idea was growing in my mind. Then Mrs Sinnott came in.

'Hello, Larry,' she said. 'Aren't you the great chap to come all this way?'

'The foolish chap, ma'am,' I said. 'I don't know what possessed me. I'm thinking maybe I should go back, and come again for Hannah in the morning.'

'Yerra, sure, you're here now,' Mrs Sinnott said. 'You'll

have some tea, and some bread and cake.'

'I won't, Mrs Sinnott, thanks. I never told my Mam I was coming. She'll murder me when I get back.'

Mrs Sinnott, a mother herself, frowned when she heard this. But then she smiled again.

'Sure you were trying to help,' she said. 'She can't hold that against you. I'll tell you what: you have something to eat, and then I'll send Matt here back with you. Youse can take one of the horses, and lead Hannah home. 'Twill be quicker. And Syl was foolish not to leave the beast up with youse in the first place. He should have recognised her.'

'Biddy Wall wasn't sure of her either,' I said. 'And she's seen her more often nor Syl has.'

But Mrs Sinnott dismissed this. 'Sure, Biddy wouldn't know herself in a mirror,' she said, 'she's that foolish. No, we'll get you home safe.'

'There's Tans out, Ma,' Conor said quietly.

Mrs Sinnott gave him a quick, sharp look. Her red cheeks paled a little bit.

'Around here?' she said.

'Up by Larry's,' Conor told her.

Mrs Sinnott recovered her colour.

'Sure, they'll head back to their barracks by dark,' she said. 'They hates being out in the dark when they're sober. They'll have to go and prime themselves with drink at least. And food, for that matter – I suppose the creatures eat, though it's a sinful waste of God's bounty.'

The mention of food reminded her of what she'd been about, and she came over and more or less made me sit down at the big kitchen table. I wasn't happy about it. The lateness and my Mam's worry weighed on my mind. And the stranger, with his military leggings and his interest in the Tans, seemed to me to be a suspicious character. The talk of 'hurted lads' was bad too. I remembered the reason that the Tans were out at all – the ambush on the Lackduf-fane road. The ambushers had to be hiding somewhere in the area, and that probably meant they were hiding on some farm. When I looked at the stranger again he was in a corner with Conor Sinnott, having a sharp conversation in very low tones. Mrs Sinnott kept casting anxious glances at the pair of them as she made me tea and cut me thick slices of freshly made bread and cake. She gave me a cold boiled egg that she took from a big dish of them. I looked at the dish. There must have been thirty eggs or more in it. Even a family the size of hers wouldn't need so many.

I muttered my thanks for the food. I was fearful, sitting there. If Sinnotts' was a safe house for gunmen then I'd rather not know about it. Even knowing nothing didn't always protect you, but it was the better than knowing too much. But I was surprised to find a prosperous family like the Sinnotts involved with the gunmen. I would have thought they liked things just the way they were.

Stephen Sinnott, another brother, came into the kitchen. He was about to say something when he saw me sitting there and stopped. He put a false-looking smile on his face.

'Larry!' he said. 'I didn't see you this long time. How is the Da keeping?'

'He's grand, Stephen, thanks be to God,' I said through a mouthful of bread and butter.

'Good,' Stephen said. 'Good.' Then he stopped smiling and went over to Conor and the stranger. He said something to them in a low voice, and the three of them went out. I didn't like the look of things here at all. I felt I'd arrived at a very awkward time. To tell the truth, I was certain the farm was full of gunmen, and any place like that was not a safe place to be. I wanted to be up and off, but it would have looked very rude to leave Mrs Sinnott's food half-eaten on the table.

Matt Sinnott must have noticed my discomfort, because he suddenly stirred himself.

'I'll go and get a rope around that cow,' he said. 'And I'll saddle the grey pony. We'll have you back home before you know it.'

And he went out too. I tried to make a respectable dent in the food, although every mouthful was harder to swallow than the one before. My mouth was dry as sawdust in spite of the tea. Mrs Sinnott made small talk, to which I mumbled responses. I wished more than ever that I'd never come. Since I had, I only wanted to be well away. Sinnotts' house had never seemed so sinister. I jumped at every noise in the yard.

Mrs Sinnott was in the middle of saying something when she stopped suddenly and cocked her head to listen. I listened too. When I heard the hoofbeats I thought first it must be Matt coming with the grey pony. But I realised immediately that that was impossible. The pony would be in one of the stables in the yard. This sound came from further away, and the hoofbeats were galloping. They were getting closer.

'Who could that be, now?' said Mrs Sinnott.

I jumped up from the table and ran to the door. I had a bad feeling about that sound. I knew people who felt things before they happened, but I don't know that was the case with me. I thought I'd just been miserable all day, from fear of the banshee and the Tans and worry about the poor lost cow, and then the threat of gunmen, even here.

When I opened Sinnotts' door I saw my father. He was on the big horse that he rode to work and he was galloping down the same slope Matt and I had walked a while before. A dim twilight had fallen, but I knew my father by the shape of him as much as anything else.

My father can't have seen it was me in the doorway, just that the door was open and that someone stood there. But he started roaring my name as he came, roaring it over and over at the top of his voice.

'Larry!' he roared. 'Larry! Come away!'

I heard people coming into the yard, and when I looked I saw maybe a dozen men there. They were all carrying rifles and pistols, and wore belts and bandoliers and all the accoutrements of war. One of them made to raise his gun but Stephen Sinnott put his hand on it and pushed it down.

'That's Johnny Quinn,' he said, which was my father's name.

The big horse was a workhorse first and foremost, but she was a game girl. She could take a ditch as well as any hunter when her blood was up. My father rode her clear down to the wall around the yard. He set her at the wall and she sailed over it, as cursing gunmen scattered, panicked, out of the way. When the mare landed in the yard her great iron hooves struck up sparks off the stones. She was snorting foam and shining with a sweat that nearly glowed in the half-light. There was steam coming off her. She didn't want to stop, and bucked and staggered while my father sawed on her reins with a savagery I'd never seen in him before. When I looked at his face I saw he looked nearly as mad as the horse. His hair was wild and his face was deathly pale.

'Larry, thank God,' he said. 'Get up behind me, quick.'

The horse was calming, but she was still dancing around. Matt Sinnott came running up, and he and Conor pulled at her bridle and stroked her.

'What's up, Johnny?' Stephen asked my father.

'Get out of it, the lot of youse,' my father said. 'The Tans are on their way here. They're gathering beyant at Moore's Cross, but they'll be coming by now.'

Moore's Cross was several miles down the road that ran

by the front of Sinnotts', but the Tans would be in their big Crossley motor-tenders.

'How many of them are there?' asked a voice. I recognised the stranger who'd been in the house.

'I didn't see. But the word is the whole country around has been sniving with them all day.'

'How do you know that they're coming if you didn't see?' the man asked him.

My father stared at him angrily.

'Don't believe me, then,' he said. 'Stay here. But let my son up behind me till we get away the hell out of this.'

'Not until I hear what's going on,' the man said. His voice sounded threatening.

'Are you deaf, man?' my father shouted at him. 'They're coming! They're coming and they'll kill every man-jack of youse. Now, let my son mount.'

Matt Sinnott looked around at the stranger.

'If Johnny says they're coming,' he said, 'then they are. We'd better scatter.'

I pushed through them till I stood in front of my father.

'We have to get Hannah, Daddy,' I said.

'To hell with Hannah,' my father said. He stretched his hand down to me. 'Get up behind me,' he said.

I took his hand and he pulled me roughly up and I mounted. I could smell the stink of sweat from horse and man, and another smell I didn't know. I think it was the smell of fear. When I looked I saw Mrs Sinnott standing in the doorway of her house. She looked terribly sad.

Somebody opened the iron gate and my father galloped away. I took one look back towards the yard and saw it full of hurrying figures, then I turned around and buried my face in the back of my father's shirt. We were well up the slope when I looked again. It was almost fully dark now. The first star was on the horizon.

I heard the sound of engines, a lot of engines. I looked towards where I guessed the road to be, but I saw no headlights. No lights showed until the shooting started, and then they weren't headlights but the flashes from the muzzles of the guns. My father stopped very briefly at the top of the slope, at the point where I'd met Matt Sinnott hardly an hour before. He looked back then, and I looked back too. There was very heavy firing coming from below. You could tell from the flashes that there were many attackers. And some of the attackers' gunflashes were coming from the east, from the open country to which the gunmen might have hoped to escape.

My father took one hand off the reins for long enough to cross himself. 'May God in his mercy look down on anyone in that house now,' he said.

Then he lashed the big horse hard with the reins and she took off like a mad thing through the fields. I don't know what way we got home. It was a nightmare ride. My father can barely have seen the walls and ditches of the fields until he was nearly on top of them, but somehow the big horse didn't kill us all. The thunder of her hooves filled my whole head, blocking out the storm of gunfire that faded as we left it behind. The jolting of the mare's gallop made me feel my very skeleton would crumble. Every now and again she'd take off in a jump, and land with a jar that each time felt as though it had broken my back. My hair was standing on end. A few times I nearly lost my grip on my father and fell off. I gritted my teeth and I cried; all the way home I cried. I tried to imagine what it must be like back at Sinnotts'; but I couldn't imagine it, and I was glad of that.

* * *

After a long time my father slowed the horse to a trot. You could feel her resist him, but even she was tired. She slowed, and he reined her in till gradually we were walking along.

'Daddy,' I called out. 'What about poor Hannah?'

'Poor Hannah be damned,' said my father. 'We've worse things nor Hannah to worry about.'

He pulled at the reins, fighting the big horse to a halt. She shivered like a mad thing as she stood, and snorted her disgust. Now in the quiet night I heard again, off behind us, dulled by distance, the sound of the guns. At least I suppose that's what it was: it sounded like someone breaking bundles of sticks. Mixed in with it were louder noises, hollow bangs that echoed in the night. They'd be Mills bombs, I told myself: grenades. They'd be grenades getting thrown at Sinnotts' fine house, and their fine Dutch barn, and their stables. And at the people in them. And at our poor Hannah. I still cried, silently.

'Daddy,' I said. 'What happened today?'

My teeth chattered as I spoke, so that I could hardly get the question out at all. Even so I could hear the whinge in my own voice, but I was too tired and terrified to care.

My father didn't answer. 'Get on out of that,' he said to the big horse, and we set off at a walk. I had no idea where we were, but my father knew. After another while he dismounted and opened a gate, and led the horse out into a lane that I knew must be our own. He closed the gate behind him and got back up on the horse's back.

'You'll help your mother pack up when we get home,' he said. 'You'll say nothing about the Sinnotts, do you hear?'

'But she'll ask me, Daddy. She'll ask me what happened.'

'She won't ask you,' my father said. 'She knows already, God help us.'

'But why are we packing? Will the Tans come after us? Where are we going?'

My father didn't answer, but set the horse to walking up the lane.

'I don't know where we're going,' he said after a while. 'But we have to go. It's not Tans we have to fear now. You just help your Mam. I'll tend to the horse and get the trap ready.'

'Can't we go in the morning?'

'No. No we can't. We should be gone already.'

I knew from the way he spoke that I'd get no more out of him. My mind was afire with terrible ideas. I was in a kind of dream – a nightmare, but a nightmare I couldn't wake up from. Things didn't seem real. We came to our house and there was only one small light showing through the kitchen window. When we went in my mother was there, sitting at the table, her head collapsed in her arms. She looked like she was asleep, and didn't even look up when we came in.

'Get up, woman,' my father said angrily. 'Are you sitting like that since I went? Have you nothing packed?'

I nearly cried out in terror when my mother raised her head and faced us. This woman did not look like my Mam at all. Her hair was dishevelled, and her cheeks scratched where she'd torn at them, and the smeared blood from the scratches was the only colour there. Her whole face was wracked and misshapen with pain and stress and grief, and it was so pale that I wouldn't even call it white. Her eyes looked plain mad, and at first they didn't even seem to see me standing there in front of her.

'Did you get him?' she asked my father. 'Did you get our poor Larry? Oh Johnny, what will we do if anything happens to him?

My father spoke to her in strong, stern tones, the way you might speak to a panicked animal, to master it.

'Don't you see Larry standing in front of you, woman?'

he said. 'Are you gone blind as well as mad? Now get up out of that and get some things together. Bring what we'll need. The rest can stay here. I'll be in when the cart is got ready.'

And he stalked out. My mother's eyes fixed on me and she gave a little cry. She gathered me up off my feet and kissed my hair and stroked me and called me pet names till I could stand it no more. This woman seemed a stranger to me. I wriggled free and stood away from her.

'Larry, my dearest, my sweetheart, my lamb,' she said.

'Mam!' I said, understanding now why my father had spoken so sternly: it was the only way to get through to her.

She stopped and looked at me, blinking her wild eyes.

'We have to pack up,' I said. 'Take what we can carry.'

I hoped she wouldn't ask me why, because even though I didn't know it, I was beginning to suspect the reason. If it wasn't Tans we had to fear, then it was other gunmen. But there was only one lot of other gunmen, and I could think of only one reason that they'd take an interest in us. But I put it out of my mind.

The urgency seemed to get through to my mother at last. She took the big old battered trunk from under the bed and started throwing things into it. I tried to think what we might want. I put a blanket on the floor and loaded it with pots and pans, crockery – a mad mix of things useful and useless, whatever caught my eye. The hurry seemed to make its own momentum. When the blanket was loaded I pulled up the edges and secured them with an old belt of my father's. Then I started loading another blanket. After a while my father came in. He told us that we had enough.

'We can't wait,' he said.

'But where are we going, Daddy?' I asked him.

'Anywhere that's not here, Lar,' he said.

He'd been so strong and sure since I'd seen him first this evening. Now the strain showed in his voice. He sounded like an empty man.

'I don't know where we're going,' he said. 'We just have to go, now, and keep on going till we're well out of this.'

'When can we come back?'

My father stood in the middle of the kitchen and looked around him at this room that his father and his grandfather had known.

'We can't,' he said. 'We can't come back.' And he sounded like he too was going to cry.

The cart was in the yard, and my father and myself loaded it up. The big horse was still sweaty and tense from her crazy gallop; but she was a game beast, and didn't protest even now at the prospect of more work.

'Will Mam be all right?' I asked my father in the yard. 'She's acting very odd.'

My father looked at me with his grim face.

'She's off her head entirely tonight with the shock,' he said. 'I suppose she'll be all right after, but I don't know. I don't know if any of us will be all right, Lar.'

We set off soon after with my Mam in the back of the cart with our belongings, and myself and my father up front in the high seat. The sky by now was overcast with low clouds, and the night was pitch black, but the horse knew the way. For a while my Mam sang softly to herself, all the old songs that I remembered her singing from when I was small. I hadn't heard her singing in a long time, but I got no joy from hearing it now.

As we went down the lane I noticed a glow in the clouds away over in the direction of Sinnotts' farm. I pointed it out to my father. He looked back to see if my mother had noticed, but she was off in a world of her own.

'That's Sinnotts' burning,' my father said.

I hadn't thought that my heart could sink any further. The urgency of the packing had driven all else to the back of my mind. Now it came back again, all of a slap, and I said nothing. After a while we reached the road and turned towards the town where my father worked. We met nobody as we drove along through the dark. At the outskirts of the town my father turned up a boreen that would take us around the houses, so that we didn't have to go through the streets and risk meeting patrols. In the darkness I hadn't a clue where we were. We might as well not have been in Ireland at all. We were just a family trekking away from trouble, with our belongings bound up in old blankets in the back of the cart and my mother sitting half-mad among them.

By now she'd stopped singing, and seemed to have sunk into an exhausted sleep. My father told me to see if she was awake, and I groped in the darkness till I found her shoulder. I nudged her gently.

'Mam?' I called softly. There was no reply except that her breathing changed a bit. I told my father.

'You should have told her you were going after Hannah,' he said. I waited for him to say more, but he was waiting for me to reply.

'It was a foolish thing to do,' I said. 'But I was trying to be useful.'

I felt his big hand on my sleeve.

'I know, son,' he said. 'I know you were.'

Neither of us said anything else for a long time, and the night was still except for the clop of the big horse's hooves and the rattle of the cartwheels on the road. Far off in the blackness a dog howled, and its call was taken up by others. The hairs on my neck prickled and I thought of the banshee Mrs Mahon had heard three nights running. Banshees were often attached to families. They came to keen over them when their time had come. Maybe the banshee Mrs Mahon had heard was attached to the Sinnotts. Maybe she'd combed her long hair and keened her keen for them, knowing what was coming to that snug old house among the trees.

'I was coming home from work and I met Biddy Wall on the road,' my father said from beside me. He spoke very quietly.

'She told me Hannah was strayed, and that you'd gone after her. "*He'll have to drive her in the dark*," she said, and I thought how foolish you were, knowing how contrary Hannah could be. So I said I'd ride out after my supper and maybe meet you on the road. But when I got home your mother was distracted.

'"*Oh Johnny, Johnny*," says she to me, "*I'm after destroying us.*" I could see she was half-mad with worry, but I couldn't get the story of it out of her for a time. She thought the Tans were after taking you off, do you see. She saw you go out, then she saw another lot of them come through the yard, and you never came back. She thought she'd find you lying dead in the field – you wouldn't be the first.'

I felt a cold and greasy feeling in the pit of my stomach. I wanted him to shut up and I wanted him to go on. Because I knew now for sure what was coming.

'She was afraid for a long time to go and look,' my father said. 'And when she did go out there was no sign of Hannah and no sign of you. So she thought they'd taken you for a hostage, the way they've done in other places. She said she fell down in the field and lost her senses altogether. She was picturing you dead in a ditch somewhere, or finding out that the Tans were going to kill you if no-one informed on them who ambushed that patrol.

'She came to herself and she went back inside and she prayed. She prayed all day. Then she saw the Tans come back through the yard again. She ran out and pleaded with their officer to let you go. And he – may God rot him – was smart. He never let on that he didn't know what she was talking about. He said he could promise nothing, but he'd do what he could – if she told him something about the men they were looking for.'

I pictured the scene in the yard, my Mam on her knees there in the dirt among the scrawny, useless chickens that we kept, with them black devils laughing at her. I felt the tears in my eyes again. How could she have known where the ambushers were? And yet she had, or she'd guessed. Everybody knew everything, I supposed, in a place like ours. Real news wasn't in newspaper headlines; real news travelled in whispers.

'She informed,' I said, in a voice hardly more than a whisper. 'My Mam informed.'

'She was stone mad with grief and fear,' my father said. 'The Tan officer played her like you'd play a fish. And when he heard what she knew then he sent runners to collect the other patrols. They were to meet him at Moore's Cross, where he'd have reinforcements. At least she could tell me that much.

'I grabbed your mother by the shoulders and I shook her. I was rough. It was the only way to get any sense out of her. "*How long ago?*" I shouted at her. "*How long ago was this?*" Because I'd met Biddy, do you see, and I knew that you'd be in Sinnotts'.'

I tried to picture that scene in our kitchen, but I didn't want to. I imagined the thoughts that must have gone through my father's head on the frantic ride across the fields to Sinnotts', with his ears straining to hear the first gunfire over the thunder of the big mare's hooves.

And all I'd wanted was to get Hannah. All I'd wanted to do was to help. My mother had informed, and that was a terrible thing. But it was I who'd been the cause of everything. Only her love of me had driven her.

'They'll find out who told,' my father said. 'Even if every man-jack of them in Sinnotts' dies tonight, others will find out. And one night they'll come for your mother. I don't know if they'd shoot her as a spy – they don't like shooting women, it looks bad in the papers. But our family is finished there for good. Nobody would so much as say hello to us. They'd cross the road when they saw us coming, and spit when they passed us. Nobody would buy from us or sell to us. I'd be an informer's man. You'd be an informer's child. And, then again, maybe they *would* shoot her. Maybe she'd be found by the road with sign hung round her neck warning others. And you and me would still be finished.'

Even in the pitch dark, even though it was miles away by now, I was tempted to look back in the direction of my home. Because I knew now that I'd never see it again.

'What will happen to the farm, Daddy?' I asked.

'I don't know. We can sell it, maybe. Or maybe we can leave it there to rot. It's rotting anyhow.'

I didn't know what to say or think or even feel. It struck me that the very last ordinary thing I'd known had been simply myself and my Mam in the kitchen, with me dawdling and her dusting: a very ordinary thing. If I hadn't been in the kitchen then we might never have noticed the Tans. All these terrible events might never have happened. When I'd walked out our kitchen door today to look for Hannah I had walked into a different world. It had looked just like the world I knew, but it had been populated by devils. I thought of the handsome Tan who'd grinned at me through the window and pointed his rifle at me. Suddenly I wished very hard that he'd pulled the trigger.

I found myself picturing the scene in Sinnotts' house earlier. All of the Sinnotts would have been around somewhere – the seven sons and old Adam. I hadn't counted the strangers I'd seen, but there'd been about a dozen anyway. That made maybe twenty men as well as the poor old woman, with her boiled eggs and bread and her big pots of tea. I remembered the attacking fire from the open country to the east: the Tans had had the place surrounded. They'd raked it with gunfire and bombed it with grenades, and it was burning now. How many had died because I'd gone looking for Hannah so thoughtlessly? How many had escaped through the dark killing fields? How many of those fine strong Sinnott sons were stretched cold now and dead, or burning with their home?

There are times when your mind can't afford to dwell on

things. Instead of the Sinnotts, I started to think about Hannah. It might be that she'd survived the attack, though the Tans would blast anything that moved – what else could they do in the dark, where any shadow might be an enemy? Was Hannah even now browsing, unharmed, by the light of the burning farmhouse? Was she running panicked with the other stock, lost in unknown fields, a terrified refugee just as much as ourselves?

My foolish thoughts were interrupted suddenly by terror. Behind me, so close that I nearly screamed, a voice was raised in a high, sobbing keen that didn't sound like any human sound. It went on and on, rising and rising, a wild, piercing, wordless howl with all the pain and anguish in it of the whole round world. The banshee! It was the banshee come to get us! I was so frightened that I nearly jumped off the cart into the road, but my father, feeling me starting to move, pushed me down. And then I realised that it wasn't the banshee. The sorrowful woman keening was my own mother, who'd given me birth, awake now in the back of our bockety cart and keening for a whole lost world of family and friends, and house and home, and maybe – for all I could tell – for our own lost poor Hannah, the poor cow.

A Note from the Author

Dear Reader,

These stories were part of a big project that I began a few years ago. The idea was to write stories on aspects of the War of Independence period that I didn't think I'd be able to fit into novels.

The original plan was completely unrealistic – to write between twenty and thirty stories covering country, town and city, and dealing with kids whose families were active in the fight as well as those for whom the entire struggle was simply a calamity. The fact that just six of the finished stories fill a whole book will tell you exactly how foolish a notion this was – I'd need to be writing till Tibbs' Eve to finish thirty such stories ... especially if I wanted to have a life as well.

The stories here are set at various times throughout the period between the end of World War I and the Truce, as follows: 'The Empty Steps' (1920); 'Mulligan's Drop' (summer 1920); 'The King of Irishtown' (1917–18); 'Dead Man's Music' (1920); 'Services Rendered' (1921); 'The Poor Cow' (1921).

None of the stories is based on any particular real-life incident – 'The Empty Steps', for instance, came from nothing more than a morning spent looking at guns in the National Museum. The germ of 'Services Rendered' was a wildly exaggerated family story told to me years ago by my Aunt Kathleen, to whom this book is dedicated. Although she came from a family of tailors, Kathleen was no great shakes with a needle and thread; but in telling supposedly true stories her skills at embroidery were incredible. According to my mother, the story as I heard it was basically a pack of lies, but I thought it was far too good a story not to rip off at some stage, so I've done it here.

Gerard Whelan

VISIT
www.obrien.ie
website

What's on www.obrien.ie?

➢ detailed information on *all* O'Brien Press
books, both current and forthcoming

➢ sample chapters from many books

➢ author information

➢ book reviews by other readers

➢ authors writing about their own books

➢ teachers' and students' thoughts about
author visits to their schools

What are you waiting for?
Check out <u>www.obrien.ie</u> today.